MOTIVE

Office Roulette, Book Two

Kennedy Layne

MOTIVE

Dedication

Jeffrey—I look forward to every day at the office, because you're by my side!

Cole—As I write this dedication, your senior year of high school has come to an end. We are so proud of what you've achieved, but also proud of what we know you'll accomplish in the future!

The Office Roulette trilogy continues with an epic battle between blame and forgiveness...

Rye Marshall had it all—wealth, prominence, and the love of his life. But nothing lasts forever, and his perfect world came crashing down around him. When the dust settled, he found himself alone and starting from a clean slate.

Grace Dorrance had made many mistakes in her life, but one stood out above the rest—an epic ending to a complex and passionate relationship. She left her former lover's life in complete ruins and tried her best never to look back at the wreckage.

Seconds chances are hard to come by, but even more difficult when Grace is arrested for a murder she didn't commit. This gives Rye the perfect motive to forgive and forget, allowing for new beginnings. Unfortunately, someone's playing a game of office roulette with everyone's lives.

CHAPTER ONE

"GRACE DORRANCE? PLEASE sign inside the box."

The police officer behind the security window slid a manila envelope through the slot. It contained her jewelry, though some pieces were expensive and some not. It was all she'd had on her person, besides the designer clothes on her back and the clip in her hair, when Detective Fred Nielsen had arrested her for murder in front of all her colleagues.

One would think that would have been the most humiliating moment of the past twenty-four hours.

Not even close.

What came while being processed for committing said murder was mortifying and had the ability to crush an individual's resolve. At least, for those who were innocent of the offense for which she had been charged.

She *was* innocent...or had been, depending on a person's outlook.

Grace had *not* taken a knife and slit the throat of her boss, no matter how many times she might have imagined doing away with him during her employment at Manon Investments.

"The box," the officer directed again rather abruptly when she'd hovered the pen over the blank space, deep in thought. "Stay inside the box."

There was no imaginary place where Grace could cover up the fact that her hands were still trembling with fear as she scrawled her signature inside the highlighted area.

Okay, so she was more than scared. She was downright terrified she'd spend the rest of her life in prison for a crime she didn't commit.

She'd been placed in a cell with other women who could have easily taken on the prison staff. They had created a dynamic where those minimum wage guards seemed like complete amateurs ignoring the fact of who was actually running the place.

It had been downright chilling.

Some of her fellow so-called bunkies had muscles in places she wasn't sure was possible. She'd done her best to be invisible by sitting in a corner and minding her own business.

"Thank you," Grace managed to say after clearing her throat of the frog lodged there. She might be horrified and on the brink of a full-blown panic attack on the inside, but damned if she'd let that show to anyone outside her own inner circle. A part of her felt disconnected, drifting on a rapid river current all alone. It was easier to go through the motions without a single defined emotion crushing the unusual fragile state she'd found herself in at the moment. "Is there anything else I need to do, Officer?"

"No," the uniformed functionary replied curtly as he took the clipboard and set it just inside the window, preparing for the next individual who made bail. Somehow, she'd been redefined as a hardened criminal in the matter of a few hours. "You're free to go."

Grace automatically turned on the heels she would have gladly given up to Bertha the Bulldog, one of the women with whom she'd shared her cell, but they had thankfully been the wrong size.

Bertha the Bulldog had eventually lost interest.

"Are you okay?" Laurel Calanthe asked as she wrapped her arms tightly around Grace, pulling her close. It was all she could do to hold back the tears that had threatened to fall ever since those cold steel handcuffs had been slapped on her wrists. It was good to have her friends close by to remind her that she could get through this with her head held high. "All that matters right now is that you made bail. We'll worry about the details soon enough, once you've had a shower and a good night's sleep."

"She *wasn't* granted bail." Justin Monroe, the criminal defense attorney who had been brought in to represent Grace, stood off to the side with his briefcase in hand. He couldn't have been much older than herself, yet he had a reputation of being one of the best peer-rated lawyers in the city. She was just happy he'd done a good job dispelling the charges against her, no matter what outrageous hourly rate he'd most likely include in his invoice. "Grace, the police were provided with proof via the parking garage's video CCTV footage that someone else had placed the bloody knife in the back of your vehicle. All charges have been dropped. You *are* free to go."

Grace wasn't sure she'd heard Justin correctly, but the round of cheers that came from her small group of friends told her otherwise. It seemed they'd all missed the catch he'd so eloquently hidden in the middle of his speech.

Had Justin just made the accusation that someone had tried to frame her for murder?

As the shock of that stark realization settled over her, Grace thought back to this morning when she'd been arrested on charges of killing her boss even though she'd supplied the police with a completely solid alibi.

Well, she'd actually fabricated that story, but Detective Nielsen didn't need to know the specifics at the moment.

All the police had to do was concentrate on the fact that Brad Manon had been killed in his office and that the person responsible was currently running around the streets of Minneapolis a free man or woman trying to frame innocent people.

What had been the motive to kill the portfolio manager of Manon Investments?

Who could have possibly benefited from his death?

Grace certainly hadn't profited from Brad's death. In her opinion, the fact that Brad had been found dead at his desk with his throat slit symbolized to her that his demise was personal. There were numerous suspects according to the police, but no one had been arrested...until today, that is.

Who would have had the audacity to try and frame her?

Better yet, who else knew that she'd lied to the police about that fateful night?

"So that's it?" Grace asked, staring directly at Justin. She'd had no choice but to tell him what really happened the night Brad was killed, but he was bound by attorney/client privilege. "I can go home and not have to worry that the police will come barging through my front door to bring me back to this hellhole?"

"That's it," Justin confirmed, though the sideways move-ment of his jaw told her that he didn't agree with her decision to stick with the alibi she'd created...with good reason. But she wasn't about to change her mind now. "It's done. You're free to go, Grace."

Laurel stepped back to stand next to Cynthia Ellsworth, who honestly looked ready to cut someone. These two women weren't simply colleagues. They were her best friends, the ones she confided in, and the two people who would bring a shovel into the middle of the woods at three o'clock in the morning with a single phone call.

Only Grace hadn't needed that shovel, and she certainly wasn't the guilty party.

"It's about damned time," Cynthia muttered, leaning down

to grab her purse from one of the chairs. "We're done screwing around here. Let's get you home, Grace."

There were still questions that needed to be answered, especially if Grace was going to sleep peacefully tonight. It wasn't a stretch to believe that a lot of people wanted to see Brad dead, such as his ex-wife or the man she'd been having an affair with over the course of the last six months. It had been thought that Meredith Manon's relationship with her ex-husband had been in good standing, but that could have easily changed when she'd started sleeping with one of the firm's key employees.

Amazing sex *did* have a way of changing people.

Grace was absolute proof of that concept, but the police didn't need to know that bit of private information. Apparently, it wasn't the only motive in play.

But someone *had* planted evidence in her car, and she wanted to know exactly who and why.

"If the police have video evidence that someone tried to set me up for Brad's murder, then who the hell was it?" Grace asked cautiously, unsure that she should be grateful to finally have this nightmare behind her.

In all honesty, it sounded like this was just the beginning of the storm that was on the horizon. But right now, she wanted nothing more than to go home and take a long, hot shower to remove the filth she'd been dipped in today. Even then, she wasn't sure she could wash away the caked-on grime of this horrible experience. Someone out there would have been perfectly happy to see to it that she was put on trial for a murder she hadn't committed.

Who could hate her so much to do such an evil deed?

"Who was it?" Grace asked, losing what was left of her patience. "Meredith? Steve? It wouldn't be surprising given that the two of them have been sleeping together."

Steve Lewis currently worked for Manon Investments as their head trader. He was good at his job, though a bit too serious and edgy for Grace's taste. There had always been something odd about the man that she couldn't quite place. Regardless, the bottom line was that he excelled at executing good trades for the hedge fund…and that was the name of the game.

But had he executed his boss because of his affair with Meredith or was that too apparent a motive for the police to pick up on?

"The video footage that was given to the police was of very poor quality, making it difficult to determine if the guilty party was even a man or a woman," Justin shared, moving all of them toward the front doors of the station.

It was like herding cats.

Grace had to wonder why she wasn't still back in her cell, considering the police couldn't verify that she hadn't been the one to put the murder weapon in her own vehicle. Thankfully, Justin managed to clear up that misunderstanding by the time they were standing on the front step of the police station.

"There was a time stamp on the tape, which proves you couldn't have been the one to put the knife in your car. It was literally the very same moment you made a purchase at the café in the lobby of the building. Thankfully, your receipt was timestamped."

It was well known among the tenants throughout the building that someone had access to the security cameras around the building that housed Manon Investments, as well as the attached parking garage. All footage on the building's video security hard drive had been erased the night Brad had been killed, but that didn't explain why the new recording that had surfaced couldn't identify the individual who had purposefully tried to frame her for murder.

"Why did the footage have such poor quality?" Grace ignored the evening chill that wrapped its cold and clammy tethers around her body. Honestly, anything was better than the stale air in that suffocating cell down in the bowels of the jail. She wanted answers, though, because something wasn't right with this scenario. "Couldn't the technical department of the police do their magic to clean it up?"

"Unfortunately, this isn't television where a computer whiz can press a few buttons and gather the evidence needed for a conviction inside an hour-long show." Justin turned to face the three women, ensuring they all remained underneath the awning and out of the cold, drizzling rain. "The owners of the building and the garage are still investigating how their security system was broken into the night of the murder. It was a commercial grade system used by a large number of corporate office buildings. It's monitored twenty-four-seven. In the meantime, they installed a backup system while their current system is being run through various tests to determine if it has any vulnerabilities to electronic interference or tampering."

"So, what you're saying is that someone knew the security system would be down this morning, yet they had no idea they'd installed a backup system with limited capabilities, and subsequently took advantage of the gap created by this unique situation." Cynthia had pointed out the obvious, but she was a stickler for crossing her Ts and dotting her Is. She was the compliance officer, after all. But her summation proved one thing—the guilty party *had* to work inside the building where Manon Investments rented their space. "Grace, the police have all this information now. It's just a matter of them weeding through the possible suspects and making an appropriate arrest this time around."

"That's our best hope." Justin didn't need to elaborate on his meaning, given that he still appeared agitated that Grace wouldn't allow him to clear up the misconception she'd purposefully given as an alibi. He held out his arm and firmly shook her hand before dropping another huge bombshell. "All costs for my services have been taken care of, but please call me should you need any further representation in the future."

"Who?" Grace blurted out before Justin could walk away. She didn't want to be indebted to anyone. Had Laurel and Cynthia forked up the money? A sliver of suspicion took hold when they both looked to Justin for an answer. "Who took care of your retainer?"

"Rye Marshall." Justin pulled up the collar of his suit jacket to protect his neck from the cold rain. He didn't seem at all curious as to why a competitor of Manon Investments would have paid her lawyer fee, but then again, it wouldn't surprise her if Justin and Rye weren't friends. Like her, Rye only hired the best of the best. "Have a good night, ladies."

Rye Marshall.

He was everything she'd ever wanted in a man, yet she'd fucked him over without either of them realizing it. And that was the sole reason she'd protected him in this case. The alibi she'd created for the night of the murder wasn't for her benefit—it was for his.

Grace would write Rye a check for the whole amount of her defense the moment she walked into her apartment. She didn't want to be beholden to him under any circumstances. She hadn't even wanted him to know that she'd been arrested, which begged the question why he wasn't here if he'd been made aware of what had taken place this morning.

"Let's get you home," Laurel said, bringing out an umbrella from nowhere and scooting closer to Grace. "Smith is around back with his vehicle, which the media has all but surrounded with cameras waiting for you to exit out the back. Unfortunately, your arrest has been splashed all over the local news, as well as the talk of the financial industry. We'll take Cynthia's car to your place, and Smith will meet up with us there later."

Grace's friends had gone to a lot of trouble to make sure that she was taken care of, and that circle now included Smith Gallo. He was one of the top analysts at Manon Investments, and also intimately involved with Laurel. The fact that the two of them had been able to make their relationship work under such recent pressure had Grace envious of their ability to do so.

Not even Laurel or Cynthia understood how heavy the baggage was that Grace had lugged around in the name of Rye Marshall. It was time she come clean, considering there wasn't any other aspect of her life that they weren't privy to under normal conditions.

"Get in the car before our ruse blows up in our faces and one of those press troglodytes figures this out," Cynthia directed in her take charge manner, firmly pressing a button on her key fob. The lights of her BMW M coupe flashed to indicate that the doors were ready to be opened. "We all need a good stiff drink after today's fiasco."

"I need a shower first." Grace ducked into the backseat, not in the mood to talk about what she'd been through at the police station. She wasn't ready to come clean about her past relationship with Rye, either, but it needed to happen sooner rather than later. Grace was surprised when Laurel joined her in the backseat instead of riding shotgun. "And you guys don't need to stay. You've been at the station all day. I'll be fine, really. I just want to take a shower and then fall into bed for a few hours."

And call Rye.

Had Justin told him to stay away?

"Fuck that shit," Cynthia exclaimed, startling Grace and Laurel simultaneously. Their friend slammed the driver's side door before pressing the ignition button to rev the quiet engine to life. "You need friends, wine, and the ability to vent. We all know that orange isn't your color."

"Orange really isn't my color."

Grace couldn't help but smile at Cynthia's attempt to inject some wry humor into the moment. Guilt had surfaced while she'd been sitting in a prison cell thinking about a future where orange was the only color choice available in the daily wardrobe for prisoners in general population.

Of course, she'd been in her street clothes the entire time today. The inmates who were there for more than a day wore orange to signify medium risk offenders. She couldn't imagine that Big Bertha would have looked good in orange, either.

"Laurel, you better have a cup of coffee waiting for me in hell when I get there, because I'm so joining you after today."

"Well, I sure as hell wasn't going by myself—pun totally intended." Laurel took the envelope that Grace had been holding and set it down on the seat. Her friend scooted toward the middle to be closer and offer comfort. As much as Grace loved her friends, it was Rye who she needed most in this moment. "And Cynthia is way worse than the two of us, so she'll actually have the key to the executive washroom."

"Hey, you don't see me stumbling onto dead bodies or potentially having a limited wardrobe choice."

Cynthia had a point.

Laurel had been the one to find Brad Manon's dead body in his office. She'd even fessed up that all she could think about in that horrible moment was her crumbling future and the fact that she wouldn't get the partnership she'd worked so hard for over these last few years.

Honestly, it was human nature to ponder how a situation could personally affect a person. Grace had said so herself, but it was a little hard to take one's own advice in moments like these. A little black humor went a long way to relieve stress, though.

And today had been beyond stressful, to say the least.

Cynthia finally shifted the car into drive and pulled out into the light traffic.

It was hard to ignore that Laurel's grim discovery had led Grace to this moment. In a weird turn of events, Grace had been on the phone with Laurel at the exact moment she'd walked into Brad's office, only to find him dead with his throat slit from ear to ear.

At first, Grace had thought Laurel had walked in on some sick joke. But as their conversation had worn on and the horror became more prevalent in her friend's tone, there had been no other alternative but for Grace to accept that her friend had walked in on the real thing. All of that had culminated into today's horrific event.

Truthfully, all she could think of at the time of her arrest was that her life was over. It didn't matter that their boss had been murdered, that his friends were mourning, or that the company was most likely going to close. A job was a job, and she'd had plenty of offers to lull her away from Manon Investments in the past.

But spending the rest of her life behind bars in an orange jumpsuit?

That was just plain wrong on so many, many levels.

And none of that had taken into account that she could lose Rye from her life all over again because of the choices she'd made…which somehow always ended up being on the wrong end of the decision stick.

The only thing she was consistently good at was her job in

settling trades for Manon Investments, as well as cultivating business relationships with the staff employed at the prime brokerage firm. She'd made a name for herself in those circles, and she didn't intend to lose her career because someone attempted to frame her for murder.

"By the way, Rye wanted you to know that he'll be arriving at your apartment sometime in the middle of the night. His plane got stuck in the Midwest due to some nasty weather." Cynthia brought the car to a stop at a red light, glancing at Grace in the rearview mirror. "We'll stay with you until he arrives."

Now would have been a really good time to come clean about Rye and their past relationship. Her friends deserved to know the truth, but she also didn't want them to think less of her.

Grace had become really close with Laurel and Cynthia after they'd all been hired by Brad, but those valued friendships had built slowly over the years. Never in that time frame had it seemed like a good time to tell them that her stepbrother had been arrested for insider trading or that he'd been the sole reason Rye Marshall had almost ended up in prison for a crime he hadn't committed.

Had Grace confided in her friends, she would have also had to admit her role in that misfortune. And she wasn't quite ready to do that, even though she and Rye were making up for lost time.

Truthfully, he had her so tied up in a mess of emotional knots that she wasn't sure what to think of him or their rekindled relationship on any given day. She should have stayed far away from him, knowing full well that the past never stayed buried among friends.

Today's events had been horrific. Beyond humiliating. And it brought back memories of a time that she'd rather forget. One thing was for certain, she would put on her best outfit tomorrow before walking through the glass doors of Manon Investments with her head held high. Rye had done it years ago, and she could do the same tomorrow.

"Hey," Laurel said softly, grabbing Grace's hand to show support. "It's over. You're in the free and clear."

"Am I?" Grace wasn't so sure, especially given that the police still didn't know about the information she'd withheld during her initial interview. "I told the police that I was with Rye the night of the murder. I lied. I gave Rye an alibi instead of telling the police the truth—that I was alone during those few hours they believe Brad was killed."

"Detective Nielsen has no idea that you lied about that night." Cynthia refocused her gaze back on the wet asphalt in front of her. "Some anonymous informant called the police with a tip that the murder weapon was in your vehicle. And it was. The detective made a hasty arrest, due to the public scrutiny on such a prominent figure in the financial industry. Now that it's been proven someone tried to set you up, the media's attention will be diverted to someone else. No one needs to know that you gave Rye Marshall an alibi for the night Brad was killed. You'll both be fine."

"You seem to be leaving out a very important detail that has nothing to do with me looking washed out in an orange jumpsuit," Grace reminded them, staring out the window and wishing she were on a warm sandy beach somewhere without a care in the world with one of those cute umbrella drinks in hand. Unfortunately, she was driving away from the police station in the cold, wet rain with a grey cloud following her every move. She wasn't so sure it was dissipating any time soon, either. "Someone *did* try to frame me for murder, which means there *is* an individual out there who knows that I didn't have a real alibi for that night."

CHAPTER TWO

RYE MARSHALL WALKED through the airport with only one destination in mind—reaching the woman who was bound and determined to be the reason he was buried six feet under sooner rather than later.

Grace was everything he'd ever wanted in a woman, but her obstinate nature would likely end with her heart-shaped ass in jail. She was damned lucky she wasn't still behind bars, given the situation and her previous reaction.

Now?

Grace Dorrance might have just placed herself in the crosshairs of a killer.

Justin Monroe had filled him in on the latest findings after he'd taken his phone off airplane mode. The suspect had purposefully planted evidence to compel the police to believe that Grace had been the one who'd killed a man in cold blood. Well, that sick and twisted asshole was about to learn that Rye hadn't gotten where he was at this point in his life by playing fair.

Rye had almost convinced himself that Grace's original fabricated alibi about the two of them being together the night Brad was killed could still hold water. After all, the damage had already been done by the time he'd reached her apartment that night to find her gone.

For him to have corrected the story she'd told Detective

Nielsen would have resulted in revealing Grace's deceit, thereby pushing her to the top of the suspect list. And that was something he refused to do…until tonight.

He had no choice now but to come forward and hope that Justin Monroe could work his same old magic with the police. All of this could have easily been erased had the responsible party not chosen Grace to be his or her patsy.

Her primary instinct had been to protect him from becoming a suspect himself. Everything she'd accomplished with her little stunt had been for naught, especially after the police found the knife with Brad's blood on it planted inside her vehicle. Thankfully, there was now proof of that via video.

"Yes, I can meet you at the station at eight o'clock tomorrow morning." Rye nodded to the familiar driver who'd opened the back door of the black town car before sliding into the backseat. His lower back muscles protested being cooped up once more, having been on an airplane for way too many hours in the last twenty-four, but this last leg of the trip would deliver him to his ultimate destination—Grace's front door. "We need to get this sorted out as quickly as possible, *and* with no further charges brought against Grace or myself for being untruthful in our original statements regarding the night Manon was killed. You said yourself that the killer had to have known that Grace didn't have an alibi or else the individual responsible would have chosen someone else to frame for the murder."

"I did my best to convince Grace to come clean after her arrest, but she refused to recant her story," Justin explained, the frustration in his voice coming across the line loud and clear. "It was by sheer happenstance that the owners of the garage put up another camera, albeit a cheap piece of shit, so that they could run various diagnostic tests on the current CCTV system. The police's IT department have been all over the building's owner and his employees. Bottom line? Grace lucked out."

"I'm heading to her place now." Rye had already conveyed to the driver the address of his destination over the phone when he'd initially booked the transportation. Honestly, he wasn't looking forward to the confrontation ahead of him, but this entire mess needed to be swept into the trash. It had taken him over a year to interject himself back into Grace's life. There was no way in hell he was allowing any outside forces to come between them now, no matter who they were or what they were willing to do to accomplish that goal. He'd had enough trouble convincing Grace that they had a future without the added nightmare of a murder trial hanging over their collective heads. "I'll explain to her what's taking place tomorrow morning. I take it her presence is required?"

"I'll pretend you didn't ask me that question," Justin said with a laugh, understanding just how difficult it was going to be to get Grace to go along with the current plan. "Good luck, man. You're going to need it with her bull-headed determination."

Rye lowered his cell phone, thinking he was going to need a hell of a lot more than good luck. He'd been relying solely on the sexual attraction between him and Grace to take their relationship further than just ex-lovers, but his fascination with her had gone far beyond the physical. He wanted her back in his life—with strings, knots, and whatever else the fuck that came along with the usual metaphors. He had a lot of ground to make up for, but this sideshow into the subsequent murder of one of his competitors had brought his plans to a grinding halt.

It wasn't that Rye didn't mourn an individual who had been a competitive opponent in the financial industry. Any loss of life was a tragedy, especially someone close to Grace. Family, friends, and colleagues would grieve, though the world wouldn't cease to spin on its axis. Those individuals surrounding Brad Manon's life would continue to move forward, paving another road in an opposite direction that was no longer affected by the choices he would have made.

Rye understood that firsthand.

"Sir?" Frank caught Rye's attention in the rearview mirror before opening the driver's side door. "We're here. Will you be taking your suitcase with you or would you prefer that I deliver it to your residence?"

Rye normally would have chosen that latter option, but he'd been awake going on twenty-one hours. In less than seven, he and Grace were due at the police station. He would need a shower, a fresh shave, and a clean change of clothes.

"I'll be needing my suitcase here. Thank you, Frank."

Rye opened his door and met his usual driver at the back of the town car. Frank had already popped the trunk and had the case in hand.

"Seven-thirty, sir?"

"Yes." Rye had already been in touch with Cynthia, one of Grace's best friends. She'd recounted the day's events in minute detail, down to the fact that Grace's vehicle had been left at the office. Both he and Grace would both need a ride to the station before parting ways for their workday. "Actually, make it seven-forty. You still like those lattes with the espresso shots?"

"Yes, sir," Frank replied with a smile, his veneers glistening underneath the street light. The man had to be in his late sixties. He was a very successful business owner, owning several town cars and employing numerous business-oriented drivers. *Professionals for professionals* was their business model. Retirement hadn't set in as well as his grey hair had, so he'd chosen to drive around a select few of his clients whom he respected and enjoyed spending time with. Well, that respect was mutual.

"Double."

Rye had spent a handful of nights at Grace's place in the past couple of months, but not many more than that. It had taken him quite a bit of time to wedge himself back into her life, not that she'd put up too much resistance. They both understood it was time to let the past stay buried. In that time, she'd shared with him her love of the café next to her apartment building. The place had the best croissants this side of Minneapolis, and the coffee was pretty damned good, too.

"Goodnight, Frank."

"Goodnight, sir."

It didn't take Rye long to get inside the building. The usual security guard was working her assigned nightshift. Her name was Cheryl Sullivan, and she was damned protective of her tenants. Rye had made sure he'd gotten on her good side and stayed there early on.

Unfortunately, Cheryl wasn't deterrent enough to protect against whoever had the steel balls to implicate Grace in a murder investigation. He'd had no choice but to call in reinforcements from a security firm, but he'd been guaranteed that Grace wouldn't notice their presence.

At least, for now.

"How are you doing tonight, Cheryl?"

"I'm good, Mr. Marshall. I'm sorry to hear about Ms. Dorrance's problems. A couple of her friends brought her home around seven o'clock this evening. They ordered takeout from one of the local Chinese restaurants, but I haven't seen any movement since then. I hope that she's alright after the horrible day I'm sure she had."

"And the media?" Rye had expected at least one or two of the news crews to be outside of the building. Had something else happened on the case to garner their attention? "Has there been any trouble with the reporters?"

Rye had also scanned the street for any sign of the security agents he'd hired to keep an eye on Grace from a distance. He'd seen neither them nor the media out front of the building. He been told the agents would be discreet until he'd had a chance to speak with Grace, but his fingers itched to call the agency's owner for reassurance. Crest Security Agency had been highly recommended and came at top-shelf price, but this special matter was regarding Grace.

Nothing was too good for her.

"There were three vans from the local stations parked outside for hours, but they left before ten-thirty," Cheryl divulged, leaning back in the black chair as her protective gaze darted over the black and white screens in front of her. She then refocused her attention on him. "I'm assuming they needed to cover something else for the eleven o'clock news, but I can give you a courtesy call before I end my shift to let you know if they return at any point."

"I'd appreciate that. You might notice another private security detail. They're on my dime. If they stand out, let me know that, as well." Rye might have to divert Frank to the attached parking garage if the media crews returned before seven-thirty tomorrow morning. The last thing Grace needed was to have it publicly outed that they were seeing one another, thus giving the media ammunition to target both of them this time around. Their pasts could very well be dug up as well, and that wasn't something Grace needed on top of all the other stress she was dealing with lately. "You have a good night, Cheryl."

Rye made his way to the elevator bank, shifting the suitcase into his left hand as he pressed the button that contained the black arrow pointing up. He could count on one hand the amount of times he'd done so in order to spend the entire night, but he relished every one of them thus far. He wasn't as optimistic about this evening's promise.

He'd already accepted that Grace Dorrance was going to be his eventual downfall.

They had met back in college, both of them young, naïve, and hungry for one another in a way that no other woman had been able to measure up to since. Those years had been the best of his life. Had anyone asked back then what their future held, he would have unequivocally said successful careers, marriage, and a small horde of crumb crunchers.

All of that had changed the moment Rye had hired Grace's stepbrother to work for him at Marshall Securities, back in the infancy of his hedge fund. Everything had crumbled to the ground the moment Brandon Walsh had been accused of insider trading, bringing the firm to its knees figuratively.

It had taken years to rebuild the firm's reputation, and even more so to restore his own standing in the community.

Never once had Rye held Grace responsible for the actions of her step-brother. She, herself, had pulled away from Rye both emotionally and physically over that following year out of misplaced feelings of self-imposed guilt. Nothing he did had prevented her from slowly fading away from his life…nothing but time could ease her own sentence.

He'd never experienced helplessness before then, and it was something he promised himself he'd never endure again, if at all possible.

The elevator doors slid quietly open, as if taunting him in his last thought.

Rye would have laughed at the irony had he possessed the energy.

He sighed in resignation and stepped into the elevator, pressing the correct floor number. He tried to rub the exhaustion from his eyes, but his attempt only made the burning sensation that much worse. He could only imagine how bloodshot his eyes must look.

"You look like shit," Cynthia said the moment she opened the door. Her biased gaze dragged over his wrinkled suit and loosened tie, but it wasn't his appearance she found offensive. It was the fact that Grace had lied to the police on his behalf, regardless that he hadn't asked her to do so...and he never would have even contemplated such a request. "You should have waited to see her until tomorrow morning. She fell asleep around an hour ago waiting for you."

Rye had met Cynthia at a few business dinners over the years, usually involving clients who invested money in both funds. It wasn't an uncommon practice. The one thing he'd noticed right away, though, was the fact that Grace hadn't told her two best friends about their past history. He didn't fool himself into thinking it had anything to do with him, and everything to do with her stepbrother's past.

"It's not my intention to wake her, so put away your claws."

He saw Cynthia's growing smile before he stepped inside and she closed the door behind him. She might not like that Grace had involved herself with Manon Investments' biggest competitor, but there was a begrudging respect for holding his own in a brawl.

"Cynthia? Is everything okay?"

Laurel Calanthe came around the corner wearing a pair of blue sweatpants and a matching t-shirt. Her hair was tousled, and she was squinting her eyes to adjust to the overhead light Cynthia had turned on in the small foyer.

Laurel had a reputation of being one of the best retail analysts on the street.

He wasn't going to lie.

He would have given anything to have her on his team, but he didn't doubt that she would become part of the new fund Smith Gallo would be opening by the middle of next year.

"Apparently, Rye didn't have anywhere else to stay tonight." Cynthia slid the security chain home before turning around to address his presence. She was taller than the other two women and barely needed to look up to address him. Her blue eyes were like lasers, but he didn't take offense at her glare. Loyal friends like this were hard to come by, and Grace was certainly blessed in that department. "You get the chair, Marshall."

Rye would have argued that his place was in Grace's bed, but he'd meant what he said a moment ago. It wasn't his intention to wake her. She needed her sleep, and his delaying the inevitable had nothing to do with the unavoidable argument in his foreseeable future.

"Have you been caught up with what happened this evening?" Laurel asked, her demeanor kinder than that of Cynthia's treatment. The women had two diametrically opposed personalities, yet the trio had formed a ring of friendship that was rare in this line of business. He did have to wonder how they would react when Grace finally told them the truth about her stepbrother's behavior, and he truly hoped they would understand her need to protect herself in this kind of industry. "Did you hear that someone planted the knife used to kill Brad into Grace's vehicle?"

"Yes, I spoke with Justin earlier." Rye set his suitcase down on the tiled floor of the foyer. They all slowly moved into the living room, purposefully keeping their tones low so that their voices didn't carry into the bedroom. A quick glance showed him the door was shut, but these walls were rather thin. "Grace and I will be heading into the police station tomorrow morning to meet with Detective Nielsen. We'll be coming clean about the timeline of the night Brad was murdered."

"Wait," Laurel said in confusion, raising her hand as she blinked several times. It was evident that she was still clearing away the cobwebs from what had to be less than an hour's sleep. "You're going to do what?"

"Grace never should have lied to the police when they questioned her regarding the events of that night. The truth needs to be told in order to flush out the guilty party. Having her in the crosshairs of someone so unstable isn't acceptable, and it's only a matter of time before he or she uses blackmail to impose on Grace to his or her advantage."

Rye easily made out that Laurel had been sleeping on the couch. Cynthia must have claimed the spare bedroom, but her quick response to his knock told him that she'd still been awake. Was she worried that whoever tried to frame Grace for Manon's murder would try something else? He wanted to assure them that the building was being watched very closely for any unusual comings and goings, but he wouldn't divulge information to them that Grace had the right to know first.

"Blackmail?" Laurel rubbed her face as she shuffled her bare feet across the floor. "Don't you think that would have already happened if it was going to?"

"Not necessarily. It's evident that someone was fully aware that Grace and I weren't together that evening. How he or she has come to be privy to that information might very well be all the evidence we need to turn this individual in to the police."

Rye didn't need to remind them that no one else knew Grace had lied to the police with the exception of the two women in front of him. With that said, he didn't believe for a moment that either one of them was the guilty party.

"Who could've known that?" Cynthia was wearing some type of lightweight robe that billowed behind her as she spun around to claim a cushion on the overstuffed loveseat. She curled her long legs underneath her, settling in for their quiet discussion. He was going to try to keep it short and sweet, because he needed at least a few hours of sleep himself to function come morning. Tomorrow might prove to be a difficult one. "Grace told Laurel and I that the two of you weren't together in the early evening hours the night Brad was murdered, but Laurel's office door was closed when she made that confession to us. Grace hasn't told anyone else to my knowledge."

Rye understood perfectly well the reason why Grace had panicked when the police had questioned her for an alibi, as they had with every employee of Manon Investments. Her concern had been for him, though, and not herself. It had clearly not crossed her mind that she'd be putting herself in between a rock and a hard place.

The original plan that night had been for Rye to drive from his house to her apartment for a late dinner, but a flat tire had delayed him by at least an hour. It didn't help his cause that he'd already been running sixty minutes behind, thus deferring his arrival well over two hours later than their originally scheduled meeting time.

To say he was shocked to discover her false confession to the police had been an understatement. They'd argued for days afterward, which eventually led them to make up in a surprisingly sexual fashion.

That hadn't prevented Grace from defending her decision, saying that he would have been the police's prime suspect if he'd had no alibi and no one to confirm his whereabouts or the reason for his delay en route to her house. In doing so, she'd unknowingly opened herself up to becoming a target for some obviously deranged individual.

"Our office doors *are* rather thin, so I suppose someone could have been standing outside in the hallway listening," Laurel proposed with obvious reservations, covering herself up with one of the blankets she'd gotten out of Grace's linen closet. He'd seen that exact same one when he'd gone searching for a bath towel last week. Laurel gripped the plush fabric as she said aloud what they were all thinking. "Which would indicate that the killer wasn't someone who Brad was in debt to or even motivated by his ex-wife. It has to be someone we are currently working with."

"Unless, of course, if Meredith Manon was at the office that day," Rye pointed out, not willing to cut anyone slack. He could tell from Cynthia and Grace's shared glances that he was right. "So, Meredith did make an appearance at the time you had your meeting."

The acute anger he'd experienced upon discovering that someone had purposefully targeted Grace had been beyond overwhelming. He wouldn't allow anyone to make her a target, and he would pull Cheryl into the police station with them if the need arose in order for her to confirm that Grace hadn't left her apartment building that evening while she was waiting on him. Yes, doing so would open himself up to suspicion, but it was better than having Grace put under the microscope once again.

"Meredith walked in on our morning meeting, but we'd assumed she'd arrived seconds before Paul started to address the employees." Cynthia twirled a strand of her black hair as she looked off into the distance, clearly trying to remember the details of that specific day. "It was the same morning when Josh Green told the entire office that Meredith and Steve had been having an affair behind Brad's back."

"That is certainly a motive for murder, now isn't it?" Rye pointed out, anxious to meet with Justin at the police station so that this piece of information could be passed along to Detective Nielsen. "Listen, we all need to get some sleep. Tomorrow is going to be a long day, and the morning is going to be a gauntlet."

"And why is that?"

Rye had known Grace was standing in the doorway of her bedroom before he even finished speaking. The heat from her stare had a way of alerting him to her presence. Not that he was complaining. There had always been something about her sexual aura that had his awareness heightened, and it had only grown stronger over the years.

Cynthia and Laurel both stood in unison and vacated the living room without another word. Again, he was astonished at what good friends they were to Grace. There were only two people on the face of this planet that he would trust with his life, and one of them was standing in front of him right now.

Grace was wearing those short shorts that he loved so much, along with a tank top that reminded him of the beloved eighties. Her blonde hair was slightly tousled, but she'd contained most of it with a scrunchy at the base of her neck. She was devoid of any makeup, which was the only reason he could see the tinted blemishes underneath her eyes that conveyed the stress she'd been under since yesterday morning.

At least he could alleviate some of her anxiety, though he wasn't sure what her response was going to be considering her moment of weakness would then become public knowledge.

He actually debated on closing the distance between them, picking her up so that her legs wrapped around his waist, and carrying her back into her bedroom to love her the way she deserved until she collapsed into a deep sleep. But delaying the inevitable wouldn't be good for either of them.

That wasn't to say it wouldn't have been a nice distraction.

The sexual tension between them hadn't been alleviated in the least during the past few months that they had begun seeing each other regularly. Hell, half the time they barely got in the door before their combined tangle of clothing was hitting the floor.

Rye would have given anything for tonight to have been in the same realm as their usual trysts. Unfortunately—and he hated to admit this—there were some things that were completely out of his control.

"Grace, I'm having Justin meet us at the police station tomorrow morning at eight o'clock." Rye automatically stood when he saw the immediate tension settle in her shoulders. He should have chosen option A. To prevent himself from closing the distance between them, he crossed his arms and remained where he was to avoid the upcoming backlash. She would no doubt fight him on this decision, but he refused to have her become a target for Brad Manon's killer. "We're going to clarify our alibis with the police and amend our statements. Our lies—"

"You mean my lie, don't you?" Grace unfolded her arms and took a step forward, her soft baby blues darkening as she harnessed the anger at his good intentions. "All you did was cover for me after you learned the truth. We should leave well enough alone. After all, I've been cleared. There's no need to rock the boat needlessly."

Rye grit his teeth at her stubbornness. Why was she always making things difficult between them? It hadn't always been this way.

"You call being targeted by a killer being in the clear? Someone obviously knows that we gave false statements to the police."

"And that someone's plan backfired, so he or she is back to square one."

"No, square one would have been you telling Detective

Nielsen the truth that night." Rye ran a hand through his hair in frustration before venturing into territory that was bound to be even more explosive than coming clean with the police, but he needed an answer to something. And he needed it now. "I've had enough of this cat and mouse game, Grace. Tell me the truth. Why are you so hell bent on protecting me when I don't need it?"

"Because I didn't protect you when you needed it the most."

CHAPTER THREE

GRACE WAS MORE than exhausted; she was downright shattered with fatigue. All she wanted was to step into his embrace, have him kiss her the way she needed to be kissed, and then make love to her until everything else around them faded into nothingness.

That wasn't going to happen.

She should have stayed in bed and ignored the low murmurs of conversation that were no doubt about her future. Well, she still had some say in how that panned out, and Rye would just have to accept that she wasn't the gullible woman who fell for her stepbrother's charms years ago.

She'd grown into an independent career woman, and one who more than welcomed the reins in the palms of her hands—she needed them.

Grace just wished they were having this discussion after she'd gotten a good night's sleep. She ran her hands over her face in hopes of lasting long enough to have the conversation she and Rye should have had months ago. Hell, make that over six months ago when she'd walked into a dinner party and saw him standing there across the room.

"Is that really what you think?" Rye asked, his disbelief evident. She wasn't sure why he would be surprised by her declaration, considering she'd been honest about why she'd left him all those years ago. These past few months they'd spent in each other's beds didn't erase their past. "That you didn't protect me from your stepbrother? I thought we'd left all that baggage in the past."

Grace sighed audibly in submission, now wishing this conversation was over with so that they could both get some sleep and start tomorrow as if it were any other normal day on their agendas. She slowly made her way over to the couch so that she had time to formulate a response that wouldn't be open to questioning. The sooner they got this out of the way, the better off they both would be.

Surprisingly, Rye didn't try to touch her as she brushed past him. They'd been acting like horny rabbits, making up for lost time. No matter how many times they had sex, whether it be in bed, up against the wall, or in the shower…nothing dimmed their sexual desire for one another.

Rye keeping his distance tonight was for the best, because her mind failed to work properly when her body came into contact with his. She needed every ounce of mental fortitude she had not to commit to something more than…what did they have?

Grace hadn't even told Cynthia and Laurel the entire truth about her past with Rye. Were they currently in the bedroom with a glass pressed against the wooden door, listening in on the conversation? She wouldn't blame them, but this wasn't how she'd wanted them to find out about her sordid past.

How could she explain that her stepbrother had traded inside information to bolster his personal portfolio at the expense of his integrity, truly believing he wouldn't get caught for his crimes?

Brandon Walsh had a side to him that was purely materialistic and greedy. It was one he'd kept well hidden, and he'd fooled Grace into believing in him. She'd been conned, just as the elderly man who had been swindled out of his two hundred dollars by Big Bertha when she'd stolen his wallet. He was just another victim of the same old game of bump and slide.

Grace had been in her thirties before her mother had married her stepfather. Hardly anyone in the business had even known that she and Brandon had been related.

Having a criminal in the family, no matter if it was by marriage, wasn't something that she liked to talk about...with anyone. And honestly, by the time she'd formed friendships with Cynthia and Laurel, too much time had passed to bring up such a delicate topic out of the blue. They probably would have choked on their wine, so she'd technically saved their lives by her omission.

Unfortunately, she'd been the one stupid enough to recommend Brandon to Rye back in the day, and all because her mother had asked Grace to put in a good word for her stepbrother.

Brandon's betrayal had cut deep, and Grace had blamed herself for Rye almost losing everything he'd worked so hard for. After all, he wouldn't have hired Brandon if she hadn't vouched for her brother's skills as a trader.

The blame lay solely at the tip of her high-heeled shoes.

"We could rehash history, but we'll only end up running in circles without being able to resolve anything more than we have before." Grace crawled underneath the blanket that Laurel had grabbed from the linen closet. The remaining warmth enveloped her, helping to chase away the cold hard truth. Or maybe that was due to actually having this long overdue conversation. Rye was right. It was better to get this over with, leaving the final decision in his hands. "I was the one who almost cost you your firm and your reputation. That is fact."

"You're covering ground that we've already gone over,

Grace. It's old news, and your take on it will never match mine. Brandon had acquired a reputation for timing the market just right in order to gain an edge for those few extra pennies that made a massive difference on most trades over one hundred thousand shares. One after another after another. He was arrested for insider trading. As far as I was concerned, that was the end of it." Rye slipped his hands inside the pockets of his black slacks. It was easy to tell he'd curled his fingers into fists, effectively showing her that he still had residual anger, regardless of his denial. "No matter how much I loved you back then, I still did my due diligence. Brandon's employment at my firm was on me, not you. You were just a reference, and one of many, as I remember it."

Grace was emotionally drained, but that didn't stop her heart from fluttering at the four-letter word he'd just uttered.

Love.

They *had* loved one another once. There was no disputing that they had something special back then, just as there was no denying now that their connection was still tethered by a simple common thread.

Unfortunately, sewing them back together meant she had to let go of the blame she carried around every second of every day. She'd thought she'd been succeeding, but then Brad's murder had put them both back in the spotlight once again.

Grace had ignored the numerous missed phone calls from her mother regarding the false arrest. They still weren't on the best of terms, mostly due to the fact that her mom and stepfather had supported Brandon after his arrest and had applied pressure for her to do the same. That request hadn't gone over as well as they thought it would, and to this day they all had a bit of a strained relationship since she'd taken it as a personal betrayal.

No, Grace wasn't returning her mother's call until all of this had blown over or Brad's killer was captured by the police.

"Are you telling me you would have hired Brandon based solely on his resume?" Grace asked, already knowing the answer from the steady tick of the muscle alongside Rye's jawline. There were some things that hadn't changed during those years they'd been apart. "I didn't think so. His failure sticks to me."

Grace could easily recall those eighteen-hour work days that Rye had put in after Brandon's arrest, the numerous phone calls to clients reassuring them their money was in safe hands, that any and all employees were being thoroughly vetted once again by a professional resource management team, and all of their references personally spoken to by Rye himself. It had been so hard to watch him drive himself into the ground all because he'd done something nice for her by hiring a member of her family.

In the end, she hadn't been able take the pressure anymore.

"I should have walked out of that dinner party the moment I saw you across the room," Grace murmured regretfully, twirling one of the tassels on the end of the blanket around her finger as she replayed that moment over and over again in her head. An old friend of hers had gotten engaged and thrown a celebration dinner with her closest friends. What Grace hadn't known was that Missy's fiancé had also been friends with Rye, resulting in both of them being in attendance. They'd been bound to run into each other at some point, but that hadn't meant she was ready to face the firing squad yet again. "Let's face it, you wouldn't be in this current situation if I'd been smart and just left that fateful night."

Rye didn't say a word to her musings, but instead removed his jacket and laid it across the arm of the overstuffed chair. His tie joined shortly afterward. Her heart began to race in anticipation, but she'd managed to slow it down by the time he'd kicked off his shoes and motioned for her to scoot over.

For a fleeting second, she thought about trying to find the energy to get up and go into her bedroom. Being near him clouded her judgement.

Hadn't that already been proven time and time again?

It was a futile effort, though, because there had been something fundamental in his demeanor since that crucial night that she hadn't been able to ignore. She could easily sense it now. It was as if he encompassed an underlying strength and belief in their relationship that she'd lost long ago, and it was downright frightening.

"Did you ever think that we might not be in this situation if you hadn't disappeared from my life the first time you ran away?" Rye yanked the blanket from her grasp and joined her underneath the warmth, pulling her close so that her head rested in the nook of his shoulder. How was it possible that everything shifted and became so...perfect? His heat soaked into her, as if to add another layer of defense against the chill that had invaded her body ever since those ice-cold cuffs had been slapped around her wrists. She gratefully slid her arm over his abdomen and allowed his strength to flood her system. "You understand that I'm never allowing that to happen again, don't you? I'm not letting you go this time, angel."

How was it that she could need him so much?

How was it that she'd lasted this long without his warmth?

No, she needed to take back those words of regret. The only remorse she suffered from was being the person responsible— yet again—for introducing the mechanism of his potential downfall.

Rye tenderly kissed the top of her head and pulled her closer, if that was even possible. She finally allowed herself to break down and release the tears she hadn't allowed herself to cry earlier, knowing full well she was safe in his embrace. She would take what he offered and then suit up for a battle she needed to win.

Five minutes tops.

That was the amount of time she would allow herself to wallow in self-pity.

Grace accepted that the fear she'd experienced about being arrested for a crime she hadn't committed had been downright horrific, but it was over now. Tomorrow would dawn a new day, and she'd be able to hold her head up high and let the world know she was innocent.

And she would continue to protect Rye in the process.

All she had to do was convince him that they should leave the situation alone. There was no need to come clean with the police about their whereabouts the night Brad had been killed. Detective Nielsen had moved on to someone else, leaving Rye in the clear.

Why muddy the waters when the suspect was elsewhere?

Suspicion would come full circle and lay solely at Rye's feet if they weren't careful on how they handled this situation.

After all, Rye was one of Manon Investments' top competitors.

Detective Nielsen would undoubtedly jump on the glaringly obvious detail that Rye's whereabouts had been unaccounted for during the exact time of the murder. He would once again be put under a microscope by the financial industry where rumors moved mountains, as well as the media circus where insinuation was almost as good as fact.

No, she couldn't allow that to happen again on her watch.

It had taken Brandon a long time to finally grow a pair of balls, fessing up to the parties that mattered that Rye had not been a part of those specific trades in question. Brandon and his lawyer had tried everything in the book to get a lighter sentence, but in the end, the truth had prevailed in spite of him.

Eventually, the SEC had cleared Rye of any wrongdoing in the matter.

But if another sucker punch was taken at his reputation?

Grace wasn't about to be the one to throw the right upper-cut, so he would just have to accept her silence on the subject. There was no need to discuss tomorrow's events now.

Grace burrowed into Rye's side even deeper, having accept-ed a while ago that he'd somehow quietly integrated himself back into her life. Not that she was complaining. She'd had years to come to terms with her role in damaging his reputation and with the reality that his firm had almost been destroyed by her stepbrother.

Growth, maturity, and time had healed a lot of her wounds. The passing years had also taught her independence, and Rye was going to have to accept that the alibi she'd given him was her way of correcting the past.

"Coffee is on the counter," Laurel said, her loud words pen-etrating the fog that had filled Grace's head. Why was her best friend talking about coffee in the middle of the night? "You have less than an hour to get ready for your appointment. Smith, you should tell Paul that we're going to be late this morning."

"Why is Smith here at this ungodly hour?" Grace mumbled, trying to grab back the welcoming abyss that had been chased away by Laurel. The blanket helped, but Rye shifted a bit and ended up taking the cover with him. "Hey!"

"We're the only ones still sleeping." Rye's tone contained that morning richness to it that she'd missed for far too long. "It's time to get up, angel."

Angel.

He used to call her that all the time before their lives had turned to shit.

Damn it.

That memory brought up the inevitable argument they were likely to have this morning.

It was like having cold water splashed into her face.

"I'm up, I'm up."

Grace wasn't sitting up literally, but she was awake enough to take advantage of the fact that Rye sat up on the couch, giving her more room on the cushions. She buried her face in the decorative pillow, inhaling deeply.

The faint scent of his cologne was still detectable.

"Smith, it's been a long time." Rye must have stood, because Grace now had the entire couch to herself. She tugged the blanket a little higher. They could all talk the morning away, for all she cared. The more time that passed, the better off they would all be. "I hear congratulations are in order."

"Here," Cynthia muttered, suddenly appearing over the back of the couch. Grace tried to groan Cynthia away, but her friend was having none of that. "It's the coffee that Laurel made, but without all the sugar and cream. Consume the required amount of caffeine so that we can all get our asses moving."

A quick peek through Grace's lashes told her that Cynthia was already dressed for the day.

Did the woman ever sleep?

It was doubtful that anyone was expecting Grace to show her face at the office this morning, considering she'd spent all day yesterday behind bars. No one would think anything of it if she were a couple hours late.

"Obviously, this wasn't how I'd wanted the announcement made," Smith said wryly, carrying on the conversation Rye had begun as if she wasn't still lying face down on the couch. "Paul has agreed to let the *no compete* clause slide, given the circumstances. I figure I'll have the new firm ready to go in around nine months, give or take."

"Are you going to take this coffee or not?" Cynthia complained, her impatience shining through. She didn't understand the people who needed caffeine to function. It wouldn't surprise Grace if her friend took the mug back to the kitchen just to prove a point. "I'm not your maid, Miss Dorrance."

Listening to two distinct separate conversations was getting a bit much, so Grace finally relented and rolled over in defeat. She took the mug of hot coffee, but she still gave it a quick glance to ensure it was black, just as she liked it. One sip enabled her to keep up with Rye and Smith's conversation.

"Are you going to bring Paul on board?" Rye asked, not moving from his position in front of the couch. Grace used her foot to nudge him to the side, so that she could wave a greeting in Smith's direction. It was the first time the man had been in her apartment. It was odd, considering that she worked with him on a daily basis and had never had an in-depth conversation with him before all their lives had gone to shit. "Or will he be a free agent?"

Smith laughed heartily, even throwing his head back as he processed what Rye was attempting with his questions. Grace had to smile, as well, given that Rye was purposefully fishing about who would and who wouldn't be available to pluck from the unemployment line once Manon Investments closed their doors.

Paul Slater would definitely be a coup, although Rye did have a good CFO already employed at his firm. Unless there was something she didn't know, which wasn't out of the realm of possibility. She and Rye rarely discussed business due to the conflict of interest.

Who was she kidding?

She didn't want to know a thing about his business. The last time she'd gotten involved had been a total disaster.

"It was just a question, Gallo," Rye shot off the warning, even garnering a laugh from Cynthia. "I have a very capable CFO, but I'm always looking for talented employees."

"I'll take that as my notice that you'll be waiting in the wings to pick up an analyst or two." Smith shared a look with Cynthia, who would no doubt stay on at the newly named firm of Gallo Capital Management. "Your warning is duly noted."

Why couldn't all their days be like this?

Sure, two men were standing in front of her leaking testosterone all over her living room, but it was better than having blood spilled at the office. At least for the moment, no one was worried about a killer, there was no stress about an impending arrest by the police, and everyone was talking about the future in a positive light. It just confirmed that she was right, and that none of them should rock the boat.

"I'll tell you what," Smith all but promised with a shake of his finger. "I'll make you a list for Christmas of who might be looking for employment elsewhere. I'll even wrap it in a nice red bow for you."

Grace was pretty sure that Rye told Smith to fuck off, but his words were drowned out by the ringing of his cell phone. He walked over to the overstuffed chair where he'd laid his suit jacket before joining her on the couch last night. It didn't take him long to answer. He listened for approximately forty seconds before speaking.

"I appreciate the heads up. Listen, if we need you to give a statement to the police, would you be free to talk with them before your shift starts later this evening?"

Damn it.

Grace kicked off the blanket and quickly sat up, trying to

catch Rye's attention. He was purposefully ignoring her, looking out the window at the city landscape.

"What did I miss?" Laurel whispered, obviously having heard Rye's side of the phone conversation. She'd stepped into the room and pulled her hair over her right shoulder. She was dressed for work, which told Grace that Smith had brought clothes and toiletries so that he didn't have to detour back to Laurel's apartment. "Is everything okay?"

"We should head out," Smith replied softly, so as not to disturb Rye. Laurel picked up on the underlying tension anyway. "We'll call Paul on the way into the office, explaining what's going on so that he's not blindsided again."

It wasn't as if Paul Slater didn't have the particulars on every single employee's alibi. He was trying to keep Manon Investments afloat until the fund could close its doors properly, and he was accountable to those clients who had put their trust in him to see it through. That included the fact that it was highly possible an employee who had access to the office building could very well be the guilty party.

Paul didn't have an easy job of it. She understood that. But he also didn't get to know every minute detail when it came to their personal lives. Laurel was involved with another employee, Cynthia had been involved with a client—*had* being the operative word, and Grace was involved with Manon Investments' top competitor. Not to mention the fact that Steve Lewis, the firm's head trader, was having an affair with the portfolio manager's ex-wife. It was the main reason Josh Green had left the firm a few weeks ago.

Josh believed it to be a stab in the back, and he didn't want to work with those kinds of people.

"Do *not* tell Paul that I lied about my alibi," Grace warned, standing up from the couch to emphasize how serious she was regarding this matter. "Rye and I need to discuss this in more depth, because it's a bad idea to go back to the police to change our statements."

"And that is our cue to leave," Cynthia chimed in, grabbing her purse and the overnight bag she'd brought with her before tossing a hand up in the air to say goodbye. The ends of her black strands brushed her contoured jawline. "Let us know what you decide. And call us if you need bail money this time."

Grace didn't find any humor in Cynthia's statement.

Laurel crossed the room and gave Grace a quick hug, whispering that everything was going to work out. Was it? Grace wasn't so sure, but she bit her tongue from arguing and did her best to find what patience she could while waiting for Rye to hang up the phone.

"Smith, I'm not sure where you parked," Rye called out right before the trio departed, "but you might want Laurel to ride into work with Cynthia. There are two media crews across the street from the building, waiting to see if and when Grace decides to leave her apartment."

"I parked in the garage, thinking that might become a problem." Smith's gaze shifted to Grace, and she suddenly got the feeling that he hadn't wanted to bring up the sensitive subject that her face was all over the morning news. "Brad's murder was the major focus on most of the business channels. I'm assuming it's the same with the local news, but there was a brief mention regarding Grace's stepbrother."

Silence hung in the air once Smith closed the door behind him, the women having already started walking toward the elevator. Grace had thought that since she'd been released, no one would dig that deep into her past. She should have known better.

The past was never buried.

She had to prevent her bare feet from running toward the door and calling back her friends, who would no doubt feel somewhat betrayed that she hadn't been truthful with them. But a bigger problem had landed at the tip of her bare toes.

Grace ignored the roll of nausea in her stomach at the impending scrutiny from her fellow employees, but she was able to push it back due to Paul's knowledge of the situation. She'd been upfront with both Paul and Brad during her initial interview. They'd all agreed at the time that no one else needed to know about her family ties to a criminal, especially given that Brandon hadn't been related to her other than by marriage.

She needed a bit more time to gather her thoughts and figure out a way to convince Rye that it was in their best interests to forgo the meeting at the police station today. They needed to let this media wave ride out its course before allowing another riptide to take effect. Surely, the police would give a statement saying that she'd been framed and that they had video footage to prove it.

"You can't hide from this, Grace." Rye had good instincts *not* to use her nickname at the moment, because that wouldn't have gone over well. He wasn't going to sweet talk her into ruining their lives for a second time. She made her way into the kitchen, all but throwing her coffee cup into the microwave. How could he not see that this would put him directly back in the spotlight? "You can't deny that it's the right thing to do."

"For who?" Grace swung open the microwave door after it signaled thirty seconds had passed. She grabbed her coffee, hoping it was enough to fortify her for the battle ahead. "Nothing we did that night can help the police catch the killer. You had a flat tire. I was here at my apartment. How does that help Brad or Detective Nielsen in any way?"

"Because lying by omission is not in our characters. Why

leave ourselves open to a lie?"

Grace had needed Rye to stay across the room. She was able to think better when he wasn't touching her, but then again, he knew that. Well, if he was going to go down that road, so could she.

"Apparently, my connection to Brandon is out for all the world to see and dissect. No one really knows that you and I reconnected, and it needs to stay that way. Now that I've been cleared, the media will hopefully move on. The media, police, and public are always looking for connections in cases like these, and they'll hit pay dirt when they figure out our history. You need to go to work and stick to your daily routine until this whole thing blows over."

"Don't you see that this gives us the advantage? Let us be the ones who control the narrative before this asshole tries to use this against us," Rye suggested confidently, taking the coffee cup from her hand and setting it gently on the countertop. He leaned in close so that the entire front of his body was touching hers, causing an instant reaction. "I know how much it bothers you to lose control of the situation."

Grace could have easily kept arguing, running them in circles until they each had to call a stalemate. Fortunately, an impasse would be in her favor, but all she could think of was that this could very well be the last time he was in her apartment for quite a while…at least until the police had caught the individual responsible for Brad's death.

"You're so mean," Grace whispered encouragingly, tilting her head back as she finally allowed him to press his warm lips against her neck. Did he truly believe that she would fall for this type of persuasion? It would have been laughable had her body not responded to his in kind. Well, it seemed that she would have to improvise and turn the tables to her advantage. She ever so slowly ran her right hand over his wrinkled shirt until she was cupping the bulge in his pants. The vibrations of his groan traveled to every erogenous zone in her body. "Why don't we think on the merits each other's positions while we take a shower?"

Rye pulled back, his smoldering gaze zeroing in on her and clearly trying to find the angle she was working in her bid to get him to see things her way. He was a very highly intelligent man. He had to see that he would lose without her cooperation.

"Are you attempting to distract me with sex?"

"Aren't you doing the very same thing?" Grace countered, purposely slipping past him and heading for her bedroom without looking back. She made sure to emphasize the sway in her hips as she walked away. "Why don't we see who comes out the victor?"

CHAPTER FOUR

R YE PRESSED HIS hands against the opposite side of the shower stall, all but forcing his knees to lock into place as Grace slowly took his cock into her mouth. The hot water had become lukewarm fairly quickly, but it was the heat of her tongue sliding alongside his shaft that kept his blood boiling. He didn't have to look at a clock or hear the sound of his cell phone continuously ringing to know she could claim the victory she'd spoken of thirty minutes prior.

"Do you need to get that?"

Grace peered up at him through her lashes, though her look was anything but innocent. Her soft hand had taken over, but the pressure and temperature weren't nearly enough to compare to her mouth.

"I swear, angel, you're—" And that's exactly what she made him do when she cupped his sac and ran her tongue over the tip of his cock. "Fuck."

He hadn't thought it was possible for his dick to get any harder than it already had, but he was clearly wrong. Grace then wrapped her index finger and thumb tightly around the base of his shaft. She only ever did that if she was trying to prolong his pleasure...or agony.

He wasn't so sure it wasn't the latter.

Somehow, Rye had enough mental fortitude to reach behind him and turn the water temperature hotter so that Grace didn't become too cold. He could have done without the added heat, but her comfort came first. Steam immediately began to billow around them, not that he cared.

Grace had taken him to the back of her throat, only to skim her lips over his throbbing cock back to his tip. Never once did she stop massaging his sac with her other hand, and the combination of sensations was enough to have him approaching his release. Unfortunately, she'd become rather a pro at prolonging that pleasure by squeezing the base of his shaft just so.

"Grace," Rye managed to say in warning, though he could barely make out her name when it came out more as a drawn-out groan of agonizing pleasure.

"Hmmm."

Her throaty vibration only made the urge to come that much stronger, but it was apparent she was enjoying herself too much for that to happen. He obviously needed to take over, because there was only so much hot water left for the remainder of their shower.

Rye desperately reached down and grabbed her underneath the arms before turning her around to face the wall.

He needed her.

He needed her in ways she could never understand, so he held her hands tightly against the tiled surface as he leaned in and caught her earlobe between his teeth as a small warning of what was to come.

"You had your fun, little one." Rye released her right hand so that he could slide his fingers down her breast, over her toned abdomen, and into her folds. The difference between her thick cream and the droplets of water running over her body was more than evident...as was her swollen clit. "A lot of fun, apparently. Were you touching yourself, Grace? Were you pleasuring yourself while you sucked me off?"

"Yessss."

Rye had pressed firmly against the sensitive ball of nerves right as she'd answered, pleased to find that he wasn't the only one on the verge of losing control.

He also needed a moment to gain a bit leverage.

"Tell me what you want, Grace." Rye licked away some of the droplets on her shoulder while lightly stroking her clit now that he had her attention. He didn't vary the pressure, even though she tried to do it herself by pressing her mound firmly against his hand. "Say it."

"Fuck me," Grace moaned, arching her back so that her heart-shaped ass pressed against his cock. It appeared that if she couldn't get him to do what she wanted with his fingers, she'd go for his dick. "Fuck me, Rye."

He'd known that their time in the shower would result in sex as sure as he knew the sun would rise in the east. It always had before, not that he was complaining. They'd both been insatiable since getting back together, making up for lost time. Even the simplest phone call saying she'd be late had him fantasizing about driving to her office and taking her right there on the desk. It had only been at her request to keep their relationship private that he'd respected her wishes and stayed far away from the office building of Manon Investments.

He reached out around the side of the curtain to where he'd set a condom on the edge of the sink, quickly tearing the foil and tossing out the ripped package after obtaining its contents. It didn't take him long to roll the latex disc over his cock and unroll it to exactly where she'd had her finger and thumb wrapped tightly around the base of his shaft.

In one heavy thrust, he was seated tightly inside of her.

The overwhelming intensity was so consuming that he was forced to close his eyes in an effort not to give into the impending release. Other than the sharp cry of pleasure that escaped her lips, neither moved as they both allowed themselves time to get used to the extreme gratification that came from their union.

Rye shifted his weight and made sure he had ahold of her hips, tilting her pelvis so that his cock would continuously stroke against her sweet spot.

"Pinch your nipples, angel."

There had been some slight changes in their time apart, but there was also quite a bit that had stayed the same. One being her love of breast play. She became so wet with just the slightest suckle on her sensitive nubs, and even more wanton when he played with them while fucking her.

She was his perfect match made in every way.

"Harder."

Rye didn't have to look over her shoulder to know that she was tugging on her right nipple, manipulating it just right to maintain the ideal pressure. The intense pleasure was driving her to rotate her hips, allowing him the ease to pull out of her until only his tip remained inside her sheath. He thrust back into her and didn't stop until they were both screaming each other's names.

Grace was resting her forehead against the tile as he finally pulled out of her, discarding the used condom and setting it near the soap dish. He'd throw it in the garbage after they finished washing each other. The temperature of the water had definitely cooled, so he turned the dial all the way to get the last of what hot water was left in the pipes.

He took a moment to himself while the strength came back into his knees, savoring the heat and steam that began to rise around them once again. Once he was sure he could function and that his thoughts were somewhat back in order, he reached for the bar of soap that held a lavender fragrance with every intention of washing every inch of her body.

"Don't ruin this moment, Rye."

"We have to face reality at some point today. As much as I loved this distraction, it's not going to prevent us from showing up at the station to meet with Detective Nielsen." Rye began to gently lather the silky soap over her shoulders and back, ignoring the annoyed glance she tossed over her shoulder at his blatant disregard of her request. "Don't give me that look, angel. You know it's the right thing to do."

Grace's blonde hair hung to the middle of her back, though she rarely wore it down at the office. He made sure to move the wet strands out of the way as he continued to stroke his hand down to her lower back. His attempt to glide over her ample ass was brought to an abrupt halt as she spun around and dug a pointed finger into the middle of his chest.

"Then don't treat me like I can't make my own decisions." Grace took the bar of soap from his hands and quickly took over the job he'd come to love again after so long. "Please explain to me—in detail, mind you—what will happen after this so-called meeting takes place."

Rye understood the point she was trying to make, but it still wouldn't change his mind that they needed to be honest with Detective Nielsen.

"The police will focus their efforts on me and the unaccounted time I spent with no one to confirm my whereabouts on the night in question," Rye explained in detail with sincere honesty, not wanting anything to stand in the way of their future. It wasn't easy to stand in front of her while she washed her breasts, her toned abdomen, and the folds he'd just been buried in until they could both hardly stand. It wasn't until she shoved the bar of soap against his chest that he continued. "But this isn't about me, Grace, and you know it. It's about your unresolved guilt—needless guilt, I might add—that you can't let go of because of your brother. What happened in the past has nothing to do with our present situation."

"You mean stepbrother. And, yes, that situation has every-thing to do with why I lied for you now." Grace grabbed her shampoo off the built-in tray and squeezed the bottle generous-ly. The lavender fragrance blended with the billowing steam, but she didn't seem to notice. She was on a roll, and he wasn't about to get flattened before he had a chance at rebuttal. "You can't just sweep what happened with Brandon under the rug as if it never occurred. It did. I encouraged you to hire him because he was my step-brother. As a result, your firm had to deal with the fallout of his criminal behavior."

"And then you ran away from me."

Rye hadn't meant for his words to be so accusatory, but that restless stirring of the unresolved hurt he thought he'd buried long ago sprang to the surface. He had never blamed her...not once. Yet, she couldn't seem to forgive herself.

"You know why I—"

"Don't." Rye had tried to be patient. He'd done his best bury his anger at her cruel actions by throwing away what they had together all because of some misplaced guilt. "We're not getting anywhere with this, so you do what you need to do, Grace, and I'll do what I need to do."

Rye whipped the curtain aside, stepping out onto the rug and not caring that the spray of water was pooling on the floor. He snagged a towel and walked out of the bathroom.

"Rye, where are you going?"

He didn't bother to answer as he dried his body off quickly, reaching for the small suitcase he'd taken with him on his business trip. Hell, he'd be dressed by the time she shut off the shower, dried off, and made it into the bedroom.

There was something about Grace Dorrance that had him blindly protecting her from anything bad happening, regardless of the cost to him. Yes, he'd worked countless of hours to reestablish his firm's reputation at the time of Brandon's arrest, but he had also been mindful of Grace's fragile emotional state over what her stepbrother's crimes had done to her family. He'd kept his own thoughts and feelings to himself, not wanting to burden her the way her mother had done in such a precarious situation.

Obviously, he'd been wrong to treat Grace with kid gloves during their past relationship.

He shouldn't be doing it now.

Rye had managed to put on the majority of his clothes and was in the middle of buttoning his cuff links when Grace walked out of the bathroom wearing nothing but a towel.

"You're not being fair," Grace accused, running her hands over her wet strands to keep them out of her blue eyes as she spoke her peace. "We were both falling apart back then, and you know it. Our lives had basically been torn in two, and we'd lost our way. We were both guilty of allowing that to happen, and I couldn't take the additional guilt of being the one responsible for bringing all of that down on our relationship. But you don't get to stand there and make it seem as if I hadn't given you ample times to talk to me about what you were feeling back then instead of staying at the office sixteen hours a day. I made the best decision for both of us at the time."

Rye could have argued with her about what was fair, because he'd let bygones be bygones from the moment Brandon Walsh had been arrested. He'd never held her responsible for her stepbrother's action, but Rye *was* guilty of not talking to her about the overwhelming panic of coming so close to losing everything he'd worked so hard for his entire life.

"You're right." Rye lifted the collar of his white dress shirt in preparation of tying his grey silk tie. He had places to go, people to see, and alibis to amend. "I could have been more open about what I was going through, and I wasn't going to unload any of my baggage onto you when you already had a full load from your family. I could see the guilt your parents were piling on you every time Brandon was brought up in conversation or when his name was splashed all over the news. I wasn't going to add to that."

Rye quickly knotted his tie and walked around her to grab his suit jacket that he'd hung in her closet. He couldn't allow himself to touch her or else he'd change his mind about what he was about to do.

"Rye, we should leave well enough alone," Grace pleaded, as if his opinion on a matter that involved him didn't count. Well, it sure as hell did. "Let's just go into work today, and then we'll sit down tonight and—"

"Angel."

Rye figured the only way he was going to get her to understand that nothing she said was going to change his mind was to resort to the intimacy they'd gained back from years of separation. It worked, but she was already shaking her head to show him that she wouldn't agree with anything other than her plan.

He couldn't do that for many reasons.

"Angel, we fucked up our relationship once. I'm not going to allow it to happen again. This time, all of our cards are going to be laid on the table." Rye shrugged his arms into his suit jacket and firmly positioned the fabric over his shoulders. He left his suitcase on the bottom of her bed and the hanger swinging on the closet doorknob. He did stop in front of her just long enough to look into her blue eyes to let her know that nothing she said or did would get him to fuck up this opportunity to have her back in his life. "I'm going to the station to speak with Detective Nielsen…with or without you. Your choice."

CHAPTER FIVE

"YOU ALL KNOW I'm the compliance officer, so I'm going to pretend that Laurel is pouring grape juice into those plastic cups," Cynthia said with absolutely no regret. Her red lips were twisted to the side, though, letting Grace know that the time had come to be completely truthful with the only two women who'd never let her down. "Everyone else has gone home, so it's just us left here in the office. Spill. How did it go down at the station?"

Cynthia kicked off her high heeled shoes as she closed the door to Grace's office, regardless that no one else was around. She most likely wasn't willing to take the chance that someone could catch them drinking at work or overhear something so private, and Grace didn't mind the added layer of protection and support considering the recent circumstances.

She'd reluctantly accompanied Rye to the station earlier once she'd begrudgingly accepted that she wasn't going to change his mind. It wasn't like she could ignore the fact that he was coming clean with Detective Nielsen, because all that would have resulted in was her being escorted back into the station with the added benefit of cuffs for misleading the police in her statement.

It had been best to come clean together.

Justin had met them downtown without having to say *I told you so* or carrying a chip on his shoulder, which was nice of him considering that she'd totally dismissed his earlier advice to do this exact thing. He'd even dealt with another detective in the room by the name of Mancini. Now that man didn't like her in the least, and neither did he appreciate Rye for not having an alibi that he could confirm. The only good thing to come from being truthful was that Rye hadn't been in town yesterday morning when someone had maliciously planted evidence in her vehicle.

Her relief had been brief, though.

Detective Mancini seemed rather eager to point out a farfetched theory that Rye could have easily hired someone else to do his bidding, especially given that he had no alibi during the timeframe Brad was murdered. It seemed counterintuitive to both Grace and Rye. Why would he arrange the murder and not ensure he had a solid alibi?

These detectives were grasping at straws.

Justin had basically taken over the meeting from there, dealing directly with Detective Nielsen. He'd smoothed over the fact Grace had lied to protect Rye, even going as far as to point out that something of this nature was a media jewel. Due to Brad's connections in the financial industry, the investigation had made national news and the governor wasn't pleased. It was common knowledge that he was putting pressure on the department to solve this murder as quickly as possible.

Justin hit the nail home when he reminded the good detectives that they really didn't want to deal with the fallout of yet another mistaken detention in the case. He pointed out that a premature arrest of an innocent woman was a black stain on the department. He suggested that they really didn't want to double down on that tactic.

All eyes at the precinct and at the office had been drawn to Grace, but she'd held her head up high just as she'd promised herself she'd do last night. No one—not even the police—were going to shame her for something she had no part in.

She'd had enough of that in her lifetime.

"Smith and Paul went to dinner with their teams of lawyers to discuss the potential merger between Manon Investments and the new firm." Laurel had already popped the cork and was pouring the red merlot they all favored over the drier white wines. Grace briefly contemplated taking the bottle, but then thought better of it. She'd left her car here overnight and would need to drive home. "Cynthia and I now have all the time in the world to hear how on earth we didn't know that Brandon Walsh was your brother. And I shouldn't have to preface that statement with the fact that none of that crap matters to us. We all have a few skeletons in the family closet, more than most in this bunch."

Laurel leveled Grace with an understanding look as the wine glasses were dispersed. It wasn't that she ever doubted their understanding, but their ring of friendship had formed slowly and there had never been a right time to fess up to being related to a man arrested for insider trading—regardless that the ties were through marriage.

"Laurel's being nauseatingly nice as usual." Cynthia took a healthy drink out of her wine glass before adding, "I'm trying not to take offense on both the professional front, as well as personal. This is not something you keep from your compliance officer, but I'm more offended that you didn't trust us enough as your friends that we wouldn't judge you for something you had absolutely no control over."

Grace took more than a healthy drink of the wine Laurel had handed over, following Cynthia's lead and kicking off her high heels.

This conversation could take a while.

"You both know I love you," Grace prefaced sincerely,

needing to get that out of the way before diving headfirst into the past. "It just became harder and harder to come clean the more time that passed. How was I going to start that conversation? Oh, by the way, my stepbrother was arrested for insider trading at the firm my former lover had originally established for high net worth individuals?"

"I find it odd you never mentioned Rye in our conversations of past lovers," Laurel pointed out, finally taking the second guest chair after carefully placing her heels underneath it. She then tucked her feet under her as she settled her small frame into the seat. "I'm not going to point out that the night I found Brad…well, I was on the phone with you, and never once did you mention that you were getting reacquainted with Rye Marshall while I was up to my hips in blood. Grace, we're here for you. Never doubt that."

"I love you both, too," Grace said softly, needing her best friends to know that her decision to withhold information had nothing to do with them and everything to do with her own insecurity. She took a deep breath and tried to sum up everything in a few short sentences. "Rye and I met when we were in college. We were young, excited about our futures, and he was beyond ambitious even then. He didn't have the best upbringing and made a promise to himself to have a better life. I was with him every step of the way."

"Did you work with him?" Laurel asked before taking a sip of her wine.

"No. Rye was just starting out, and I thought having a secure position with benefits at a larger firm would be better for my stability. It's funny. I hadn't wanted to mix our personal life with our professional life, but then I ended up offering him my stepbrother on a silver platter." Grace leaned her head back against the headrest at her naivety back then. It was astonishing how many years had passed, yet it seemed like only yesterday. "It all went to hell after that."

Cynthia tilted her head and studied Grace, her blue eyes missing nothing.

"You blamed yourself, didn't you?"

"Wouldn't you?" Grace asked with a humorless laugh. "The SEC came into the office like tanks making their way across the battlefield. Rye was lucky to have anything left to salvage by the time the authorities got done with their investigation. He was working at least sixteen-hour days and sometimes more to do what he could to convince his clients to keep their money in his hedge fund. In the end, I couldn't continuously watch him go through something so horrendous knowing I was the one responsible."

"He didn't blame you." Laurel had made the accurate assumption, but Grace sensed her friend understood that a relationship that strained never would have made it past a year. "That was many, many years ago, Grace. How did the two of you hook up again?"

"You remember when that old friend of mine had that engagement party a while back? Well, I had no idea that her fiancé was friends with Rye. One thing led to another, and here we are back where we started."

"I get why you felt the need to give Rye an alibi, Grace. I really do, but I highly doubt putting yourself at risk is something he would condone." Cynthia twirled her wine glass, nodding her head as if she'd just made a realization. "No wonder he wanted this entire situation resolved quickly."

"Don't take his side," Grace warned, pointing a finger in desperate need of a manicure Cynthia's way. "You're my friend, and you should be supportive of my decisions. I almost destroyed his career and firm once, Cynthia. I wasn't going to allow that to happen again when I was the one he was driving to see the night Brad was killed."

"Oh, don't be selfish." Cynthia wasn't known to avoid confrontation, and she could always be counted on to tell the truth. Grace usually wasn't on the receiving end of those skirmishes, though. "Did you ever imagine how Rye would feel if your ass went to prison for a murder you didn't commit, all because you had some misplaced guilt over something that happened years ago? See? It sounds even more ridiculous to me when I spell it out."

"What Cynthia is trying to say is that your good intentions could have backfired very badly, leaving Rye to shoulder the guilt of your poor decisions." Laurel shot Cynthia a disbelieving glare, who shrugged her shoulders and took another sip of her wine. "Honey, try looking at it this way. Rye would have gone through the same exact situation that you went through, but this time you would have done it intentionally."

Grace continued to sip her wine as she allowed the advice of her friends to finally penetrate through the barriers she'd had in place ever since she'd walked out on Rye. Their so-called friendly intervention had the effect they'd wanted, but that didn't mean Grace's mindset could easily be turned over with a few words. What she needed right now was to be with Rye.

Of course, when had recent events ever gone her way?

The unexpected crash of what sounded like a glass falling to the floor echoed throughout the office, even with the door closed. Cynthia and Laurel were out of their seats and setting their wineglasses down, both of them telling the other to be quiet.

"You said no one was here," Grace whispered with unease, quietly setting her bare feet on the plastic floor mat underneath her desk chair.

"No one *was* here," Cynthia whispered back, leaning down and grabbing one of her high heels off the carpet. She hastily waved toward the phone on Grace's desk. "Call 911. Right now."

"911?" Laurel quickly glanced back at Grace. Her friend's facial expression was one of doubt. "Do you know what that's going to look like if it turns out to be Steve, Vern, or some other employee? Three overreacting women, that's what."

"Laurel's got a point," Grace pointed out, opening her top desk drawer to pull out an envelope opener. "I really don't want to be front page fodder for the newspaper tomorrow morning. Blair mentioned to me earlier that she had to work late. Are you sure no one was in the office when you came in here?"

"Of course, I'm sure. I can't be caught having wine in the office," Cynthia muttered as she made her way to the door. "I promise you there was no one here. Call 911."

"What do you think you're doing?" Laurel quickly stopped Cynthia from reaching for the doorknob. "And what the hell do you think a high heel is going to do? At least Grace has a sharp object."

"Have you seen these things?" Cynthia asked, holding up one of her Jimmy Choo heels. "This sucker can take out an eye at thirty paces. Besides, all I need to do is reach my office."

"Why? Do you have a bat in there or something?"

"My firearm."

"Your what?" Grace quickly joined her two friends, having grabbed her cell phone so that she could run if need be while calling 911. Besides, she wasn't going to allow her friends to confront a possible murderer alone. "Now who's keeping freaking secrets?"

A strangled cry of pain was muffled by the closed door, but it was enough to have Cynthia making a hasty decision. She twisted the knob and was out into the hallway before Laurel could stop her.

"911, what is your emergency?"

Grace managed to relay the most critical of information as fast as she could, given the circumstances. Laurel had already followed Cynthia out of the office and to the left, which was the direction from where the sound had originated from.

"Please hurry," Grace murmured the plea as she observed Cynthia raise the high heel over her head as she quietly tiptoed into the foyer. She left out that the scene before her resembled a horror movie gone bad. "I think—

"What the hell are you doing?"

"Shit!"

"Gun!"

"Everyone stop what they're doing," a firm voice ordered, causing all eyes to become glued to the man and woman standing in the glass entrance of the office. "We're with Crest Security Agency, here to protect Grace Dorrance. My name is Ethan Chambers, and this is Taryn Chambers. Ma'am, are you alright?"

The ma'am turned out to be Marilyn, who was standing behind her desk and staring in horror at the firearm being pointed her way. The petite blonde holding her weapon slowly lowered it to her side, taking in all four women and the situation at hand.

"Grace, are you on the phone with the emergency response services?"

Grace realized that Ethan was asking her the question, and she automatically nodded.

Security agency?

Here to protect her?

She hadn't hired anyone for protection.

"Let me take this from here," Ethan said reassuringly, a confident smile doing just that. The woman he was with quickly and efficiently made her way over to Marilyn, the firm's receptionist, who was currently still standing behind her desk holding up an arm that had a trail of blood trickling down the side of her hand. "Operator? This is Ethan Chambers with Crest Security Agency. There's been a small mishap and..."

Grace took a seat next to Laurel, who'd claimed one of the cushions on the couch against the far wall. The petite blonde named Taryn was currently speaking with Marilyn while wrapping her hand in a paper towel and cleaning up the blood spilled from apparently trying to pick up a piece of broken glass.

"Well, looks like Rye has some explaining to do," Cynthia said, joining the other two women on the couch. She still had the high heel clutched in her hand. "I mean, seriously. Do you two not talk to each other at all outside of sex?"

"Cynthia's right." Laurel leaned her head back against the cushion and closed her eyes. "You two need to sit down tonight and come clean with one another. I don't think I can take anything else without going into cardiac arrest. And I'm young. I work out. I shouldn't be having these heart palpations every time I come into this office."

"Here you are," Ethan said as he handed the cell phone over to Grace. "I apologize for any confusion, but we were on the other side of the elevator bank. We were aware that Marilyn had returned to the office. Unfortunately, when we heard the sound of glass breaking, we didn't want to take the chance that someone, somehow, hadn't slipped past us. It wasn't our intentions to disturb you or your peers."

"I forgot to forward the phones to the automatic voice system." Marilyn's tone was shaky, but Grace could totally understand why. Taryn had escorted Marilyn to one of the two chairs that matched the rather uncomfortable couch the other three women occupied. "My arm accidentally bumped into the coffee cup tray. I didn't mean to cause so much trouble."

"You did nothing wrong, ma'am," Taryn assured with a smile, diverting her attention to the three women on the couch. "Could one of you tell me the location of the first aid kit, so that I can clean up Marilyn's cut? It doesn't need stitches, but a butterfly sterile strip couldn't hurt."

"I'll show you."

Laurel patted Cynthia's knee as she stood up, leading Taryn through the trading room and toward the small office kitchen. Grace was still focused on Ethan, who was currently on his own cell phone and obviously sending a message to someone…who was no doubt Rye Marshall.

"Rye hired you to keep an eye on me, didn't he?"

"Don't take that tone with him," Cynthia warned in a soft and controlled manner, totally aware that Ethan could hear every word she said. "You have to admit that it's probably a good idea considering someone tried to frame you for murder."

"You'll have to take that up with Mr. Marshall." Ethan clipped the cell phone into its holder attached to his belt. The shoulder holster he had on underneath his lightweight jacket told of another item he was keeping close to his side. "Once we get Marilyn cleaned up, we'll go back out. You won't even know we're here."

That was so far from the truth, it wasn't even funny.

"You should probably have that talk sooner rather than later," Marilyn said, leaning forward while holding her hand in the air. She cast a sideways glance Ethan's way, almost as if she didn't want him to overhear what she had to say. "Your face was splashed all over the early evening news channels, as well as your stepbrother's mug shot. By the way, did you know that he was released from prison last month?"

CHAPTER SIX

"YOUR MOTHER OR stepfather didn't contact you about Brandon's release? I know I heard you on the phone with your mother right before my last trip. I find it very hard to believe she wouldn't have told you something of that significance."

Rye moved around his kitchen with ease, though the tension from this evening's events still hung in the air alongside the delicious fragrance of the omelets he'd just served onto two plates. He had no doubt that Grace hadn't eaten a thing today, especially after this morning's tense meeting with Detective Nielsen.

Grace was currently sitting at the kitchen table and twirling the glass of orange juice he'd set in front of her, apparently not having heard a single word he'd said over the last five minutes. Her beautiful face hadn't lost the frown she'd had since he'd shown up at her office after Ethan Chambers had called him during a business dinner earlier this evening.

"Grace?"

"I get why you felt the need to hire a security agency to watch over me. I really do, but I think you should have a team assigned to you, as well. What if it was Brandon who killed Brad? What if he was setting me up this entire time? Let's face it. Everything makes sense with his recent release in mind. He probably holds a grudge against the both of us. Especially me, because I refused to sit in the courtroom beside my mother and stepfather when Brandon was sentenced, as if I could somehow condone his criminal activities."

Rye returned to the stove to set the pan on one of the back burners, surprised at which road Grace's mind had decided to drive down considering how upset she'd been with him after their meeting with Detective Nielson. How was it that she'd contained the situation in a box and made an assumption that everything revolved around her stepbrother?

"Brandon committed insider trading and served out his sentence, but I highly doubt that he's become a cold-blooded killer, Grace." Rye walked back to the table and snatched the orange juice from Grace's hand. She sat back against her chair, crossing her arms and shaking her head emphatically at his statement. They both needed something stronger than juice and coffee. "Either way, you have a point about security for the both of us. We're fine tonight since you're staying here with me, but I'll contact Crest Security Agency in the morning."

"I'm surprised you're not at the office making calls after the breaking news about our relationship and what happened with Brandon." Grace picked up her fork and used the side of the prongs to cut into her omelet. He noticed that she didn't take a bite as he poured them both a glass of red wine. "I'm sure that kind of salacious news story has reached your clients by now."

Rye lifted the glasses from the counter and joined her at the table. They were treading on shaky ground, though it was pulverized soil they'd already covered a time or two. He decided another vehicle was best for the terrain.

Without a word, he gently took the fork out of her hand and lifted the small amount of food to her mouth. Grace hesitated before parting her lips and taking his offering. Their stares remained connected as she slowly chewed and swallowed the only meal he was good at making.

"You're more important to me than any of my investors, Grace." Her blue eyes dilated as she inhaled a deep breath through her nose. It was clear she hadn't thought he'd steer the conversation to their relationship. But wasn't that where all roads led to in the end? "I'm not sure if I ever told you that. I thought you should know that up front."

"Rye, you don't have to—"

"Tell you the truth?" Rye cut off another bite of the omelet and ate it, giving himself time to say what he should have said years ago. "This morning, once we began arguing, it was like being taken back in time. We used to fight over what the other wanted to do or say before storming off and not giving a damn about the consequences. You joined me today, though I figure you believed you didn't have much of a choice. The thing is, angel, none of this matters—not Brandon, not your mother, and certainly not our careers."

Grace was about to reply when he slipped in another bite of the omelet. He grinned when she grabbed the napkin and pressed it against her lips. He'd bought himself maybe ten seconds, tops.

"We let outside influences dictate the directions of our lives. Aren't you about ready to open the sunroof and take the wheel?"

Grace surprised him when she remained silent. She reached for her wineglass, taking a healthy sip and leveling him a curious stare over the rim of her glass.

"You can let the past slide away as if nothing happened? The news coverage doesn't bring up bad memories?"

"I *can* let the past fade into oblivion, and what the media is currently covering is old news," Rye replied, leaning back in his chair and taking her lead by reaching for his wineglass. "I hate to break this to you, angel, but you're the only one standing in our way."

Grace continued to drink her wine while studying him, allowing the soft jazz music he'd put on in the living room to make its way into the kitchen. He'd bought the Victorian style home around two years after Grace had left him, though he hadn't recognized at the time that he'd decorated the place with subtle designs and color schemes that she would appreciate. The two-story home even had the wraparound porch she'd always admired on other older homes they would drive by on the way to visit her parents.

"What if I were to tell you that—"

The light melodic ring of Grace's cell phone drifted from its place on the table, preventing her from finishing her sentence.

"You should get that," Rye encouraged, easily recognizing the offended look on her face. The only person who could ever garner that type of distaste was Gail Walsh. "Seriously, find out what your mother has to say and why she felt the need to keep Brandon's release from prison a secret from you."

"This isn't a conversation that's going to go well, especially once I throw my own two cents down that well."

Grace sighed in agitation, but she grabbed her phone and took both it and her wine into the living room. Her sweet perfume hung in the air as her bare feet silently made their way across the kitchen tiles. A quick glance at her plate told him that she hadn't eaten nearly enough to keep her healthy, but he doubted she would finish her meal after the conversation she was about to have with her mother.

Rye finished his omelet before he wrapped her plate in saran wrap and set it on the middle shelf in the refrigerator. He hadn't yet heard Grace raise her voice, nor did he hear her crying…both a good sign.

He was about to grab the bottle of wine and join her in the

living room, thinking maybe she needed more sustenance in the alcohol department, when his own cell phone rang.

"Jag. Is everything okay? I thought you were overseas."

Jag Douglas. His brother in every way it counted except blood. But blood meant nothing in the long run. Loyalty trumped everything else in Rye's book.

The two of them had grown up in foster care, learning faster than most that they only had each other to rely on. No family, no matter their good intentions at adopting a child, was going to take two eleven-year-old boys into their home when infants and toddlers were available from either their own area or another country.

"I heard about Brandon Walsh." The connection that had been established for this call wasn't that clear, and static cut off some of Jag's words. The mention of Brandon was enough for Rye to know that this was a checkup call. "...you okay?"

"Let's say I was surprised to find out he was released, but things are fine on my end. There's been no attempt at contact." Rye hadn't spoken to Jag in quite a few months. Hell, the last time Jag had reached out from some ship in the middle of the Indian Ocean, it was before Rye and Grace had gotten reacquainted. "Listen, Jag. You should know something."

"That you and Grace Dorrance are back together?" The signal had suddenly become clear, as had the doubt lacing Jag's worried tone. He'd been there when things had gone to shit. "You sure you want to go down that road again, brother?"

It was funny that he'd compared the path he and Grace were on to rough terrain earlier, and here Jag was pretty much referencing the same image. That's how similar the two of them thought. It was a fact that would never change, and that particular constant meant the world to Rye.

"I'm more confident about Grace than I was when we were

staying at Mrs. Lagasse's place in St. Paul and I told you it was a bad idea to take her car to Cocoa Beach. You didn't listen to me back then. Hell, you've never listened to me."

"Well, I'm hearing you loud and clear now," Jag said, rich laughter following his words. "You and Grace, back together again. Go figure. Don't be a fucking idiot this time. Talk to her, spend time with her, and for the love of God…don't let that prick come between the two of you ever again."

"That's advice I can willingly take, brother."

These phone calls that Jag made from a deep-sea exploration out in the middle of nowhere didn't last long, so Rye switched the topic back to Jag and when his ass was due back on land. The last minute of the conversation was spent talking about the renovations of Jag's newly acquired fixer-upper and what equipment and supplies were needed to be delivered to the warehouse property they both had an interest in. Rye promised he'd take care of it, knowing it was too hard for Jag to set up from a vessel halfway across the world.

"I'll see you next month. Email me the specs on those parts."

Rye had been leaning against the counter when he disconnected his call, giving him the ideal location to notice Grace standing in the doorway. Her glass of wine was empty, her arm dangled at her side with her cell phone in hand, and the color had drained from her face.

"What's wrong?" Rye asked in immediate concern, wondering what the hell Gail Walsh had said during that phone conversation to cause such a reaction. He took a step forward but stopped midstride when the doorbell rang. Her disbelieving expression told him she was fully aware of who was at the front door. "Grace, what is it? What's happened?"

"Brandon was brought in for questioning tonight in the murder of Brad Manon."

CHAPTER SEVEN

"HOW DID YOU know Brandon had been brought in for questioning?" Grace took the wineglass Rye had refilled into the living room, joining Laurel on the couch. Both she and Smith had shown up at the door the moment Grace had told Rye the most recent news. "I appreciate you coming to tell me in person. Unfortunately, my mother beat you to the punch in her own way."

"Smith received a courtesy call from Detective Nielsen. They have an arrangement."

"It certainly pays to have the family connections, doesn't it?" Grace asked, though her sincerity came through loud and clear. Smith's father was a well-known and respected judge, giving Smith an inside track to this investigation. "Does Cynthia know?"

"I gave her a call on the way over here."

The roaring fire Rye had built in the fireplace was flickering in all its glory, but Grace couldn't feel the warmth of the flames. She'd been cold ever since her mother asked if she'd go down to the station to show her support for Brandon. Gail Walsh truly believed in her stepson's innocence in spite of everything, but Grace had already reached a guilty verdict hours before.

"You're not going to believe this, but when I discovered that Brandon had been out on parole for over a month...my first reaction was that he could have murdered Brad. I mean, no one else I could possibly imagine would have a reason to frame me for murder."

"I wish I could say I'm glad the investigation is over and that we can return to our lives, but that's not the case, is it?" Laurel reached over the middle cushion and rested her palm over the back of Grace's hand. "What are you going to do?"

"I'm going to let the police handle the case and figure out where my future is headed from here."

Grace hadn't realized it before tonight's events, bit it was Rye who had lucked out in the family department. He had Jag Douglas…a brother Rye could trust with his life. They'd both grown up in foster care and only ever had each other to rely on.

Who did she have, besides her two best friends, who she considered closer than family? Her mother had invested all her time and energy into a marriage that had been based more on money and security than love. Nothing Richard Walsh or his son did could take Gail's eyes off the prize—more wealth than she'd ever dreamed of in her entire life with Grace's birth father.

"Is Rye part of that future?" Laurel asked, her approving gaze skipping over to the entrance of the kitchen. "It's obvious that he loves you very much."

"You know, we used to say those three words to each other all the time back before our lives were blown to pieces by the very man who just tried to pin a murder on me."

"I don't know if this will help or not, but Brandon is claiming innocence."

Laurel rested an elbow against the back of the couch, seemingly giving Grace's stepbrother a shadow of a doubt.

"Are you kidding me?" Grace understood that it was impossible to describe in minute detail the hurt and anger that Brandon had put her through with his past history of criminal activities. There was no remorse back then for doing what he did, and there wouldn't be now. Only excuses and claims of innocence. "Laurel, Brandon Walsh made my life a living hell. He all but destroyed Rye's career."

"Hey, girl, I'm behind you one hundred percent. You know that. All I'm saying is that the police made a hell of a mistake when they arrested you yesterday morning. And wouldn't it be better if Brandon was actually innocent? You don't want this crap destroying what little of a relationship you have with your mother. She won't have anyone."

"My relationship with my mother was left in tatters when she sided with Brandon the first time this kind of behavior surfaced." Grace took another healthy sip of the red wine, contemplating going to get another bottle. But alcohol wouldn't help erase the sense of abandonment she'd experienced during the call with her mother. "I'm beginning to realize how much I hurt Rye when I left him high and dry after the trial."

"And you're wondering how he can so easily forgive, aren't you?"

"Yeah," Grace replied softly with recognition she should have acknowledged months ago. "I am."

"Then I'll take that as our cue to leave. You two need to talk."

Laurel collected her wineglass and the red high heeled shoes she'd worn to the office that day and walked around the coffee table. As if on cue, Smith appeared and the only woman he had eyes for was the beautiful brunette walking his way. Their intimate connection was palpable, and Grace couldn't be happier that her friend had found someone who considered Laurel his entire world.

Rye was quietly standing off to the side, but his dark gaze wasn't on the couple in the small foyer. He was observing her with a quiet stillness that took her breath away. A round of goodbyes commenced until Laurel and Smith had taken their leave, leaving only the rhythmic clicking of the antique clock tucked into the corner of the living room.

"Why did you allow us a second chance?"

Rye's question came out of nowhere.

Had he and Smith been listening in on her conversation with Laurel? It was doubtful. Neither one of them were the kind of man to do so, and they both held their sense of personal honor over just about anything else.

Either way, Grace wasn't sure how to respond. Anything she said in this moment would give him the upper hand. Her emotions were raw and tattered, and she was likely to say things she couldn't take back...like the truth.

There was only one thing left to do until she was ready to sever the last string to her heart before she surrendered her will to his.

Grace slowly unfolded herself from the couch and gently set her wineglass on the coffee table in front of her. One by one, she began to unfasten the buttons on her blouse as she gradually walked toward the blazing fire. The sheer curtains most likely weren't enough to prevent someone from seeing what was taking place inside the house, which was why she couldn't stop the small smile from spreading on her lips when Rye killed the lights. That one simple action reduced the atmosphere around them to dancing shadows of yellows and oranges cast off from the flickering flames.

They both wanted each other all to themselves.

The tempo of the flames seemed to synchronize with the barely discernible music, encasing them in a small circle in the center of the room. Someone would have to be literally standing at the window to catch them in such a compromising position.

The security agency Rye had hired was still in position

somewhere just beyond the visual line of sight with the house. Professionals were paid to keep out of view. They surveyed the likely avenues of approach once they'd secured the primary residence. They wouldn't be looking this way. The agents would almost certainly be released from their duties tomorrow morning, seeing as Brandon was about to be behind bars for the murder of Brad Manon and his failed attempt to frame his stepsister.

Grace allowed all of those thoughts to disappear the instant her blouse hit the floor. There was no room for the past in this moment. She and Rye had been given a second chance, and she wouldn't allow herself to throw it all away like she had the first time.

No, she was going to savor every word, every touch, and every moment.

This was their time, and no one could take it away from them.

"This is the second occasion today that you're using sex to avoid talking about the past." Rye leaned against the doorframe, not even attempting to reach for the buttons on his dress shirt. The fact that his gaze had lowered to the pink lace covering the ample flesh of her breasts told her that he wasn't too bothered by the delay. "I'm beginning to feel manipulated."

"If you come over here, I'm sure I can comfort your bruised ego."

Grace slowly unzipped the pencil skirt she'd worn to the office today. Within seconds, the matching lace and delicate silk of her underwear were visible. This particular set of lingerie were among his favorites.

She lowered herself to the plush rug in front of the warm fire, relishing the heat that emanated from the hearth in waves. The logs crackled and threw embers into the air, reminding her of the electricity between the two of them. Not even the years that passed had diminished their attraction for one another.

"You're playing with fire."

"I believe you already set one," Grace reminded him, not referring to the contained inferno beside her. She laid down on the rug with one raised knee slightly open to let him know that she was his for the taking. "Don't tell me that you're afraid to get burned."

There was something beyond sexual to watch a man take the time to unbutton the cuffs of his dress shirt with measured patience. Power and wealth were aphrodisiacs, but to then add confidence to an exceptionally gorgeous specimen of a man...well, it could cause a woman to melt with one longing glance.

"When have you known me to be afraid of anything?"

And then you ran away from me.

The weight of his words from earlier this morning reverberated in her head, but she quickly dispelled them. She'd hurt him, but she wasn't blind. They both had the ability to destroy one another.

Love was more powerful on a battlefield than hate, but it was trust that evened out their playing field.

He had trusted her enough to take her back, and she trusted him not to seek revenge for her ill-conceived premise that they could escape the fire they created.

"I'm afraid," Grace admitted softly, raising her arms above her head with her wrists together in complete surrender. He would understand the significance of her gesture. They'd always played around in the bedroom before, vying for dominance. But this time, she was completely his. "Be gentle with me, Rye."

Grace held her breath when he began to unbutton his dress shirt, revealing his broad shoulders and defined biceps. Seconds later, his undershirt was gone. Her gaze settled on the contours of his chest. Those types of muscles weren't acquired in a gym. They were from hard work he'd put into restoring his beautiful home, which he'd claimed he bought with her in mind.

She didn't doubt him for a second. This house was right out of their previous discussions of dream homes, right down to the gabled Victorian style roof.

"Take off your bra and panties."

There was something downright naughty when a man—this man—gave her directions. Her heart raced and arousal traveled through her spine in anticipation of what was to come.

Grace arched her back and unfastened her bra, taking her time removing the straps from her arms. She was busy enjoying the view in front of her and didn't mind delaying in the least. By the time she'd removed her lingerie, he was standing there in the nude.

And what a stunning sight he was to see.

He was already hard, his cock long and wide. There wasn't a time her sheath didn't burn in its attempt to accommodate his generous size. A dull throbbing began to pulsate inside of her, anticipating the inevitable.

Rye dropped to his knees, but instead of lowering himself over her, he grasped her ankle and slowly raised it to his lips. He pressed a gentle kiss on her sensitive flesh while maintaining eye contact.

Her heart skipped a beat.

"Take your nipples in between your fingers and don't stop rubbing them until I tell you to."

Grace moaned when she realized what he was about to do, and her contribution would only have her reaching that precipice in a matter of minutes.

She'd wanted this moment to last.

"Rye, you know that I'll—"

The light nip on her calf was a small warning, but it was enough to tell her that he wanted her complete surrender tonight.

Grace didn't have to touch her nipples to know that they were already hard, but she took them between her index fingers and thumbs anyway. Delicious, tiny shocks of stimulation blossomed throughout the ample flesh as she began to knead the delicate nubs. Her back immediately arched as the pleasure became overwhelming.

He'd done this to her before, but she still emitted a cry of primal desire when he slid his fingers through her folds.

"You are so wet," Rye muttered, almost as if he were talking to himself. His deep, rich tone was like molasses being poured over her body. She wasn't expecting him to slide a finger inside of her, so she couldn't control the small contraction that gripped him tight. "I don't want you coming yet, Grace. And I don't want you to stop pinching your nipples…not until I tell you to."

Grace was beginning to lose all the worrying thoughts that plagued her throughout the day. The only thing that mattered in this moment was the pleasure he was giving her.

Rye continued to gradually stroke his finger in and out of her entrance, purposefully ignoring that sweet spot he'd found so many times before. He was prolonging her pleasure, yet he didn't seem to care that the delay was agonizing.

And he didn't stop there.

He placed his other hand on her inner thigh, letting her know he wanted her to separate her legs even wider. She obliged, knowing full well what he intended to do. She couldn't hold back the loud cry that escaped her when his warm lips surrounded her clit. It was impossible to hold back his name when the tip of his tongue stroked over the throbbing tissue.

The pulsations of her erogenous zones were now timed together, and her arousal rose every time she squeezed her nipples.

"I need to come, Rye," Grace managed to gasp, perspiration beading on her flesh...not from the fire, but from the overwhelming pleasure he was giving her body. "I'm going to come."

"No, you're not."

Rye continued to lightly stroke her clit with his tongue until the indulgence began to mimic the flames in the fireplace. There was a burning need that couldn't seem to be placated, yet continued to reach for complete and utter dominance. Her nipples were no longer separate from her core, and she began to float away into that sheer oblivion she'd only ever reached with him.

Her soft fingers continued to do his bidding, not stopping their manipulations of her nipples. Her breath hitched with each tight compression. The strokes of his finger that was still eluding her sweet spot caused her hips to rock on their own. Inherent response had taken over, and there wasn't a thing she could do about it until he allowed her to come.

Grace screamed again, but this time it was when his touch disappeared. It was as if ice cold water had been splashed over her soul, and not even the fire next to them could do a thing about the change of temperature.

"Rye, please," Grace pleaded, finally opening her eyes to find him above her. He'd quickly rolled a condom in place. She didn't have time to brace herself when he drove himself into her with one thrust. The burn that accompanied his possession was now an out of control inferno. "Yes!"

"Come for me, angel."

Grace broke into a million pieces.

Rye had seen to it that her calves were on his shoulders,

allowing him full access to her in the most vulnerable way possible. He was balls deep inside of her, and she wouldn't want it any other way. His cock finally satisfied that itch that had settled in her sweet spot from the moment he'd unbuttoned the cuffs of his dress shirt.

Flashes of light burst in front of her as she tried to maintain eye contact with Rye, but her body was in full blown meltdown as wave after wave of pleasure washed over her. Her lashes finally closed to savor her release. He'd joined her in the fall, and together they rode out the tide until they were mere puddles of bliss.

Grace was hardly ever aware of how she ended up in his tender embrace, and this time was no different. She was on her right side, facing the fireplace with her back against Rye's solid chest. Her still hardened nipples were cold in comparison to the heat from the flames in front of them.

"You have no reason to be afraid, angel," Rye murmured, pulling her in tighter against his body. "I would never let anything happen to you."

"I know," Grace whispered, allowing the fatigue she'd been fighting since her arrest to finally claim her consciousness. There was something she needed to say before she fell into that welcoming void of slumber. "This isn't a second chance, Rye. I loved you back then, and I still love you today. Nothing has changed, and I was foolish to think I could ever live without you."

CHAPTER EIGHT

"WHY ARE KURT and Goldie still parked across the hallway?"

Grace came up short when Cynthia sidled up next to her, both of them on their way to Laurel's office. A quick glance out the glass doors and through the outside foyer explained the inquiry.

"Ethan and Taryn are still my protective detail until Rye decides to stop paying them," Grace replied wryly, having already had this argument on the drive into work today. "He says he's not convinced Brandon is the actual killer or is guilty of anything to do with murdering Brad."

"But you think he is?"

"Absolutely, beyond a shadow of a doubt." Grace had seen her stepbrother in action, just as Rye had. He was erring on the side of caution. She wasn't sure why he would take Brandon's plea of innocence to heart when he'd stooped to the same kind of criminal behavior before and turned out as guilty as sin. "And don't think I didn't notice the pearls around your neck. I take it Gareth is coming into the office today."

"I'm wearing pearls because they go with this outfit. Nothing more. Gareth has nothing to do with the choice of jewelry I wear."

"You keep telling yourself that," Grace countered as she was the first through Laurel's office door. "Cynthia's wearing pearls."

"I heard Gareth was stopping in to speak with Paul and Smith." Laurel looked up from the financial reports on her desk with a perfectly arched eyebrow. "When are you going to accept your fate, Cyn?"

"Bite me," Cynthia muttered, taking one of the guest chairs. She conveniently changed the subject. "So what's the word on Brad's office? I heard Paul and Smith were thinking of renting office space on Fifth Avenue."

"I bet Gareth would like to bite you," Laurel countered under her breath, but she allowed Cynthia to change the subject. "And yes, Paul and Smith believe that we should have new offices if we're going to have a new name on the door."

Laurel's sights landed on Grace, suddenly changing the topic of conversation for a third time in the span of ten seconds.

"You professed your love for Rye Marshall last night, didn't you?"

"How—"

"Oh, please," Cynthia interrupted with a wave of her hand and a twitch of her red lips. "You're glowing like the next bride-to-be. It's almost nauseating, but I guess you could have done worse."

Grace had to laugh at their banter and welcomed the light-hearted discussions about their love lives, as well as their careers, with open arms. It had been weeks since they'd been able to have small talk in this manner. It was about time their lives got back on track.

"Did you notice that Steve has the same clothes on as he did yesterday?"

"Marilyn told me a few minutes ago that Meredith called in to speak with Paul twice this morning," Grace said, wishing she'd stuck around the receptionist area to hear more. "You'd think that Steve and Meredith would be relieved that the police have a prime suspect, especially given that the police had been focused on their affair as being the prime motive for Brad to be killed."

"Someone had access to the building's video surveillance equipment," Laurel pointed out hesitantly, sharing a look with Cynthia. Grace couldn't believe that either one of them were even doubting her stepbrother's guilt. "We're not saying that Brandon didn't do this, Grace, but you have to admit there are still some loose ends to be dealt with."

"Do you think I haven't thought about—"

"Grace, Detective Nielsen is here to see you."

All three women stared at Marilyn as if she'd just announced that Saks OFF 5th was having a fifty percent off sale.

"Did you just say that the police are here?"

"Yes," Marilyn replied hesitantly, sneaking a glance down the hallway. "I heard him say they released your stepbrother this morning."

Marilyn's bomb was kind of a dud, considering that Grace had expected Brandon to have great representation since his father was footing the bill.

"The media is probably having a field day," Grace muttered, standing from where she'd been leaning against the wooden filing cabinet Laurel had positioned against the far wall in her office. "Fine. I'll speak with him."

Grace followed Marilyn out into the hallway after reassuring Laurel and Cynthia that this was most likely a courtesy visit from the police. After all, she'd been framed for murder and the person responsible had just been released from questioning.

"You were right about the media," Marilyn conveyed in a low voice before either one of them reached the foyer. "Marshall Securities and Manon Investments have been the sole focus on the financial channels. Steve's been glued to the television since he arrived this morning."

There were two large screen TVs in the trading room, allowing the traders and staff to monitor the day's events. Technically,
the news regarding Rye's connection to her had broken
yesterday. Add in Brandon's trip to the station for questioning,
and who knew how the media would spin her involvement.

The loose end that Laurel had brought up regarding someone having access to the building's security system lingered, and
Grace couldn't help but stop Marilyn right before they entered
the foyer.

"Marilyn, what's going on with Steve today? Did something
happen between him and Meredith?"

Marilyn sighed the way she usually did when it came to company gossip. Nothing happened in this office without Marilyn
knowing about it, though she was usually discreet with whom
she shared that information with—unless asked. She leaned in
close and began to spill today's latest chatter.

"Before your stepbrother was on the police's radar, Meredith
supposedly asked Steve if he had anything to do with Brad's
murder."

Grace gave a low whistle of surprise.

"That couldn't have gone over too well with Steve."

"Meredith has been calling Paul all morning, wanting to
dump her shares of Manon Investments." Marilyn shook her
head in remorse. "It's truly sad, because the two of them were so
happy together."

Grace didn't want to rain on Marilyn's parade of happily-
ever-after sagas that the woman seemed hell-bent on relishing in
her day-to-day gossip mill. Yes, Steve and Meredith had gotten
together after Meredith's divorce, but to get involved with one
of her ex-husband's employees hadn't been the wisest of ideas or
too discreet, either.

"Ms. Dorrance, thank you for meeting with me," Detective Nielsen greeted, holding out his hand in offer. He gestured back over his shoulder. "I see from the presence down the hall that you still have personal protection. That's reassuring."

"Why do you say that?" Grace asked before realizing that having this conversation out in the open wasn't the best of ideas. "Before you respond, let's take this to my office."

Grace didn't offer the detective a cup of coffee, already knowing that Marilyn had taken care of such formalities. Neither one of them said a word until they'd reached the privacy of Grace's office and she'd closed the door.

"It was my intention of calling you first thing this morning after your stepbrother left the station, but his lawyer is every bit as good as your Justin Monroe." Detective Nielson took a seat in the first guest chair that didn't have folders covering the fabric. He unbuttoned his suit jacket as if he intended to stay awhile. "And the reason I believe maintaining additional security is so important is because of what happened before, and so it doesn't happen again."

"Then you believe that Brandon is guilty?"

Detective Nielsen took too long to reply. His brief silence set her on edge, which was obviously his intention.

"Your attorney said it himself yesterday morning," Detective Nielsen pointed out, resting his elbow on the arm of the chair. "The governor wants this case closed quickly, and the prosecutor felt there was enough evidence for me to formally question Brandon Walsh."

"Why are you here then, Detective?"

Grace had slept like a baby last night, and it wasn't only because she'd been physically satisfied. It was also with the knowledge that her stepbrother was about to be behind bars and could no longer damage her reputation. This courtesy visit suddenly didn't seem so chivalrous.

"Who else besides Brandon Walsh would want to see you put away for murder?"

Grace leaned back in her chair, grateful that this questioning was being done on her turf. This office was her sanctuary. This place of business was her domain. She could handle anything thrown her way, even the disbelieving notion that Detective Nielsen had doubts about her step-brother.

"No one," Grace answered confidently. "Brandon was guilty all those years ago for insider trading, and he's looking for payback after spending all that quality time in your gladiator academy. Are you telling me he has an alibi for the night Brad was murdered?"

"Like you did?" Detective Nielsen countered, bringing Grace up short.

"I guess I deserved that." Grace could graciously admit when she was in the wrong, not that she'd intended to do so until her arm had been twisted. "But I also have a security guard in my building who can vouch that I never left my apartment that evening. At least, not until I received Laurels' call. I'll be honest, Detective Nielsen, It's beginning to sound like I should have my attorney present."

Grace held up a hand, foreseeing exactly where Detective Nielsen was headed with his next statement.

"Rye was already running late that night before having a flat tire," Grace acknowledged, but she wasn't going to stand back and allow that bit of information to cloud what was right in front of them. "And my answer is still the same—no one else has any reason whatsoever to frame me for murder."

"Rye Marshall almost lost his business because you recommended your stepbrother as head trader for his firm," Detective Nielsen pointed out, purposefully ignoring the fact that she'd already asked and answered his question. "Fast forward so many years, and Mr. Marshall is presented with a gift-wrapped situation where he can out the two people who tarnished his reputation."

Grace bit the inside of her lip to stop herself from overreacting. Detective Nielsen wasn't an obtuse man, and it was more than apparent he was following up on whatever bullshit story Brandon had spun while he'd been in custody.

"I can see that Brandon has filled you in on quite a bit of my history with him, as well as Rye." Grace reached for one of the pens on her desk. Holding the writing implement gave her something else to do besides escort the detective out the door. It was best she used this visit to her advantage to ensure there was no doubt as to her stepbrother's guilt. "I'm sure you've looked into Brandon's past interrogations regarding the insider trading charges. You'll see a pattern of him shifting blame onto other people. Don't be fooled again, Detective Nielsen. You have your suspect. It's time to close the loop."

Detective Nielsen didn't break eye contact, but his brief nod told Grace that he was satisfied with her explanation. She would have sighed in relief, but unfortunately, his next statement told her what the problem was with preventing the book from being slammed on this case.

"Brandon Walsh didn't have access to the security room in this building, nor does he have the knowledge to hack into such a sophisticated system."

"Brandon spent years behind bars with his fellow criminals," Grace pointed out, refusing to back down and give the police any shred of doubt when it came to her opinion about her stepbrother. "You have no idea what he could have learned in prison during that time."

"Detective Mancini is currently looking into that as we

speak," Detective Nielsen shared generously, allowing the tension in Grace's shoulders to somewhat recede. "I appreciate you taking the time to speak with me, Ms. Dorrance. It cuts through a lot of red tape, which I've been up to my neck in ever since this case landed on my desk."

Grace didn't need to have Detective Nielsen explain his last statement. He wasn't used to dealing with financial firms, their employees, and the vast amounts of money and top tier attorneys who came with such criminal charges. It most likely wasn't in her best interest to speak without Justin being present, but her decision had certainly sped this process along.

"I just want my life and those of this firm to be able to put this behind them." Grace stood when Detective Nielsen decided to take his leave. "Should you have any other questions regarding Brandon Walsh and the lengths to which he'll go to in order to cover his own ass…I'm only a phone call away."

Grace waited for Detective Nielsen to close the door behind him before she basically collapsed in her chair. She'd been upfront with him and blatantly honest. No one else besides Brandon had reason to try and frame her for murder, and Rye being the responsible party wasn't even a remote possibility.

But it did beg the question—how had Brandon taken down the building's security system?

CHAPTER NINE

R YE WASN'T A man who liked to be kept waiting, but that was exactly what Grace was forcing him to do now.

He'd all but promised her that he wouldn't show his face at Manon Investments, for obvious reasons. The firm was basically his competition when it came to courting high net worth individuals, so it wouldn't look good to have him visiting an employee who handled the settlement of trades.

He didn't give a shit.

"Rye, what the hell are you doing here?" Grace asked with incredulity, having looked up from the papers in her hand and caught him standing in the doorway of her office. "Are you crazy? We talked about this. The media—"

"The media knows that we're involved, so there shouldn't be a problem with me visiting my lover at her place of business."

"It's a problem for me, because you're also this firm's major competitor."

"Then come work for me. No more conflict."

"Rye, I'm not having this conversation while I sit here at work." Grace rolled her chair back and stood to her full height. She was downright beautiful, but he held his tongue. He'd yet to address her declaration of love from last night, and he sure as hell wouldn't do it here in such a sterile environment. "I told you on the phone this afternoon that I had to work late."

At first, Rye thought she'd been avoiding the continuation of their discussion last night. She'd declared her love and loyalty to him before falling asleep in his arms. He hadn't had the heart to wake her, but it sure as hell hadn't been his intention to wait twenty-four hours before finishing what she'd started.

"The market closed at three o'clock central time, at which point the employee in charge of *my* trade settlements was done an hour after that. As a matter of fact, he's already had dinner with his family and is most likely sleeping in his recliner watching the evening news with the remote still clutched in his hand." Rye took a step into her domain and closed the door behind him, having noticed that the head trader was still hanging around the office at six o'clock at night. No one else needed to hear his and Grace's private conversation. "I'm beginning to think either I'm not paying my staff enough or they're just not as dedicated to their jobs. I'm also trying not to take offense at the fact that you just intentionally turned those papers over, as if I would take whatever information is on them and use it for my own gain."

"It's not what you think," Grace said with a sigh that spoke volumes about her frustration with the day's events. She'd told him about Detective Nielsen's visit on the phone this afternoon, which had resulted in a slight argument about the fact that she hadn't called Justin to be in on the impromptu meeting. "I've been wracking my brain on how Brandon could have accessed the building's security system. I told Detective Nielsen to follow up on Brandon's time in prison, but…"

Grace's voice trailed off as she struggled to admit that her stepbrother's plea of innocence might actually ring true. Rye hated seeing her struggle with this, and it was the very reason why he hadn't called Crest Security Agency to pull their agents.

Someone had gone to a lot of trouble in his or her attempt at framing Grace for murder. There wasn't a chance in hell he was gambling with her life until he was one hundred percent certain that the guilty party was behind bars.

"What is it that you've been doing here then?" Rye asked, closing the distance to Grace's desk. He didn't miss the way she pressed her fingers to her right temple. "Did you at least take some ibuprofen for your headache?"

"Nothing is getting rid of this headache, Rye." Grace slowly reached for the pen she'd set down on top of the paper, removing the only obstacle preventing her from flipping the sheet over. "And now I have guilt layered on top of my doubts. It's not a good combination."

Rye had already figured out what she'd written down on the piece of paper before he ever picked it up from the glass top of her desk. Sure enough, a list of names of every Manon Investment employee was printed neatly under two columns—cleared and not cleared.

"I see you've gone outside the employees of Manon Investments." Rye didn't take his eyes off the list as he made himself comfortable in the only guest chair available. The other one was filled with files. "Gareth Nicollet? I'd heard he was out of the country at the time of the murder."

Rye found it very telling that his own name was not on the list, and neither was Laurel or Grace.

"Gareth wasn't in the country, which is why I've put him in the cleared column." Grace sat down before rubbing her hands over her face. There was something she wasn't sharing with him. "Did I tell you that Gareth threatened to kill Brad a week before his murder?"

"You and I both know that his words were hollow hyperbole." Rye continued to skim over the names she'd written down on the numerous lines. One thing stood out. "Do you truly believe that anyone you've listed here would try and frame you for murder?"

"If the responsible party thought for a second the police were closing in on them…yes. I believe that desperation can cause people to do some shitty ass things."

The only time Grace ever used foul language on a continuous basis was when she was either pissed at the world or frustrated over something she couldn't figure out. In this rare case, it was for both reasons.

"And whoever was that desperate would have had to have known that you didn't have an alibi that night."

"But I did," Grace pointed out, reminding him that the security guard at her building had recently given a statement to the police. "I have a witness that states I never left my apartment that night."

"You're assuming the guilty individual thought things through to that extent, but you said yourself that you were here at the office when you disclosed that you'd lied to the police."

"Which brings me back to Meredith." Grace leaned forward on her desk and pointed to the paper in his hand. "It always comes back to Meredith."

"We've already informed Detective Nielsen that Meredith might have overheard your conversation. The police have all the evidence regarding—"

"Detective Nielsen pointed out that once Brandon was paroled from prison, you then were given the opportunity to take out the two people responsible for what happened to you all those years ago."

Grace wouldn't have worked herself up into a frenzy and created such a list if something hadn't happened to cause her to doubt Brandon's innocence. Rye had known all along that Detective Nielsen had said something that upset her this morning. Now that he was armed with that bit of information, he had the tools to dismantle her stress.

"Angel, you haven't put anyone on this list who Detective Nielsen doesn't consider a suspect." Rye held his tie against his shirt as he stood and set the paper back down on her desk. Their problem didn't lie in the fact that the police were looking elsewhere besides Brandon Walsh. Unfortunately, it meant that Nielsen thought Brandon was being set up. "I'm not worried that the detective is questioning my motives. There's a reason I hired the best of the best. Justin Monroe will handle any questions the police may have, while you and I carry on with our lives."

"Carry on?" Grace had pushed her chair back when Rye walked around her desk only to use the hard surface for something to lean against. "We can't move forward until this is taken care of, Rye."

"Did you tell me that you loved me last night?"

It was clear that Grace hadn't expected him to bring up her declaration of love, but he also saw the deep-seated fear in those blue eyes of hers.

"Yes, I did."

Damn it.

Rye didn't want to start their newfound relationship while she was terrified to have it ripped apart into shreds by another outside source. Neither one of them were qualified to investigate people, but he'd pick apart each name one by one if going through the list would give her some sense of peace.

He pushed himself off the desk and removed his jacket before walking back around to the guest chair he was about to become quite familiar with over the next hour.

"I'm giving you sixty minutes before I throw you over my shoulder and take you home." Rye grabbed the piece of paper before she could, holding out his hand for the pen she was hoarding to herself. "I really don't want to reciprocate my feelings in my competitor's main office."

Grace's perfectly outlined lips tugged at the corners, but her relief was palpable.

"Every single name on here had the means to commit Brad's murder. We're looking for motive." Rye clicked the end of the ballpoint pen so that he could write down the motivation of each suspect. "Meredith was having an affair with Steve. That gives each of them motive."

"But Meredith and Brad were divorced, so that takes away their motive."

"No, it doesn't," Rye countered, recalling something she'd said after the day she'd come clean with Laurel and Cynthia about him not having an alibi. "You mentioned that Joshua Green had gone to Brad hours before he was murdered to expose Meredith and Steve's affair. If Brad still had feelings for Meredith, I can guarantee you that he would have found a valid enough reason to fire Steve."

"So both Meredith and Steve still had motive, regardless of their denials."

"Why *is* Steve still at the office?" Rye asked, leaving the paper and pen on the desk when he leaned back in his chair. "Does he usually work this late?"

"Meredith asked Steve point blank if he had anything to do with Brad's murder."

"Ouch. That would definitely put a hitch in his giddy up." Rye had a sudden revelation that the woman in front of him had never doubted for a second that he'd had nothing to do with his main rival's murder. He'd never given her faith a thought, because he also had that much faith in her. Hell, she believed in him so much that she'd fabricated an alibi so there wouldn't be suspicion cast on his name. "Meredith doesn't love Steve."

"No, she doesn't," Grace answered softly, having obviously

guessed where Rye's thoughts had gone. "And that alone would give Steve Lewis motivation to kill the man she did love."

Rye glanced down at her handwriting on the paper, choosing another name that didn't seem to fit the suspect list.

"Vern Roberts."

Rye was wondering when the man's name would come up in conversation.

"We always promised one another not to cross personal and professional lines." Rye carefully studied her body language to see if this put a dent in their faith in one another. He was once again floored that she didn't seem to be batting an eyelash where this situation was concerned. "Vern came to me two months ago, looking for a fresh start. I know that he's basically Paul's right-hand man. I would have been a fool to turn Vern away without hearing him out."

"Fresh start?" Grace frowned and shook her head at what was obviously still not public knowledge. "Rye, Vern is on the board. There's no way he was looking for a fresh start, nor would he do that to Paul. Besides, Vern has too much invested in Manon Investments."

"Grace, come on," Rye said with a shake of his head. One thing Grace wasn't? Naïve. "You said yourself that Brad had changed over the last few years. His dismissive attitude was setting people on edge, and everyone knows that Paul had lost control of Brad a long time ago. It was only a matter of time before the percentage on your employee turnover rate began to climb. Hell, even Smith was leaving Manon Investments in the very near future."

"There's a bit of a difference between an employee jumping ship and one who has a vested interest in the firm," Grace pointed out, still seemingly somewhat dumbfounded that Vern had been the one to seek out Marshall Securities instead of the other way around. "When Steve brought up the subject of Vern having been offered a job at your company, I automatically assumed that you had reached out to him."

Rye could understand why Grace and the others here at Manon Investments would have thought that was the case, but the truth now made Vern a prime suspect.

"You think something else happened between Brad and Vern to make him seek employment elsewhere," Rye suggested, leaning forward on his chair and scribbling down a note next to Vern's name. "Detective Nielsen is fully aware of my business handling with Vern Roberts, so my guess is that he's already been cleared."

"And you know as well as I do that the police have been following leads given by the real killer, such as trying to frame me for murder and then leading the police to Brandon."

"So you're saying you don't think Brandon is guilty," Rye shot back, finally getting to the crux of the matter. Grace had put hours into this list, because there were names included he recognized in the business that had nothing to do with Manon Investments. "And you don't like second guessing yourself."

Grace groaned in frustration and pushed on the desk so that her chair slid backwards on the plastic mat beneath her heels.

"I wasn't second guessing myself until Laurel and then Detective Nielsen pointed out that Brandon doesn't have the knowledge to hack into a security system. I mean, what if they're right? Detective Nielsen is under no obligation to continue investigating this murder if the prosecutor thinks he has enough to make the charges stick against Brandon."

Rye loathed the fact that the killer had involved Grace into his or her grand scheme, but there was one thing she could do to ease her conscience.

"Angel, grab your purse." Rye left the list of suspects she'd come up with on her desk. He highly doubted that she would want it thrown away, at least until she was convinced the right man was behind bars. "We're going to grab a bite to eat, and then we're going to go pay your brother a visit. You were the one who recognized his guilt the first time around when he was claiming to be innocent. There's no reason you can't do the same tonight."

CHAPTER TEN

G RACE SAT NEXT to Rye in silence as he drove them back through the city from her parents' residence to his place. She wasn't sure what she'd expected to happen, but it certainly wasn't to be turned away at the door by her mother.

"This will pass," Rye reassured her, reaching over the console of his Audi and taking her hand. "Your mother is hurt because you wouldn't go to the police station when Brandon was initially brought in for questioning."

"Brandon wasn't only being interrogated over a murder rap, but he was also brought in to be questioned about framing me for a crime I didn't commit," Grace pointed out unforgivingly. Shock had been the first emotion she'd undergone while standing on the front step of the Walsh's two-story home in Edina. Their wealth was displayed for all to see in the landscaping, let alone the long driveway that led to their sterile mansion. "My mother acts like Brandon is this innocent child who needs protecting, and I'm over it. Done. I'm her daughter, damn it."

Her shock had eventually turned into anger about a mile outside of Edina.

"I can't believe my own mother told me to get off her property," Grace muttered in contempt as she stared at the red light Rye was slowing down for near the crosswalk.

"I'm sure it didn't help that I was by your side. I imagine she still holds some animosity for me." Rye squeezed her fingers in support, but he didn't seem to realize that his statement made her mother's reasoning all the more fucked up. "Maybe you can—"

"Don't you dare say I should go back alone in the morning," Grace said, cutting Rye off mid-sentence. He understood more than most what loyalty meant, especially given the fact that he'd only kept one man around from his childhood...and that was Jag Douglas. "And you being with me should have been incentive to let us in, because it would have given Brandon a chance to apologize for what he did to you in person."

Resentment of the unfolding events coursed through her veins, but it gave her clarity over what needed to be done.

"You said yourself that Detective Nielsen is good at his job, but I think you should talk to him again—with Justin present, of course." Grace held her breath, hoping that Rye would do as she suggested. She hated that the police thought Rye was involved, and she didn't doubt that Brandon had spun the situation in that direction. He must have explained that to her mother, because that's the only reason Grace could come up with as to why she'd been turned away tonight. "We need to provide a united front. This way, Detective Nielsen isn't wasting time investigating either of us."

"Two hours ago, you were making a list of suspects," Rye pointed out as he pulled the Audi into the parking garage attached to her office building. A stream of headlights from behind joined them, indicating that either Ethan or Taryn had been following at a close distance. "Vern was at the top, along with a few other employees who we haven't even discussed— such as Blair."

"Blair?" Grace had been the one to write the names down, and Blair had been at the bottom of the suspect pool. "She was underneath Steve, Meredith, and Vern. What do you know about

Blair that I don't?"

Rye didn't answer right away, which meant he'd been with-holding information.

"Rye?" Grace waited for him to pull his car into the slot alongside hers. He had an early meeting up in Duluth, which meant he'd be using his car service. She'd wanted her own vehicle to drive into work tomorrow. "Why would you think Blair had reason to kill Brad?"

"She wouldn't, as far as I know, but that doesn't mean she shouldn't be thoroughly vetted," Rye countered, shoving the stick shift into park. His gaze zeroed in on the rearview mirror, most likely to ensure that their protective detail was back in place after having come through the entrance of the garage. "Blair had an affair with Paul before she ever came to work at Manon Investments. It's old news, and most likely has nothing to do with this case."

Grace honestly couldn't see Blair and Paul together in such an intimate fashion. Blair was in her mid-twenties. Paul had to be in his late forties. It made no sense to hire someone after sleeping with them, knowing full well the future could be ripe with problems of a personal nature.

"Blair was twenty-two at the time," Rye said, filling in the blanks. "They were both adults, and she'd been at another firm before he ever offered her a job at Manon Investments. Paul hired her because she's good at her job, not because they cared for one another."

"How do you even know this?" Grace asked, unable to be-lieve that Rye could have this kind of knowledge when it had been so well hidden from the employees at her own firm. "This industry is starting to rival the plot of an afternoon soap opera."

"Blair's brother works for me," Rye admitted, though he was still cryptic on how he'd discovered such a bombshell. They'd agreed this second time around to never allow business into their personal lives. "Listen, we have our own jobs to do. Nielsen isn't coming after me. Arresting you was a major mistake for the police department. Having Brandon all but served up on a silver platter could make any seasoned detective wary, and Nielsen is just crossing his Ts and dotting his Is."

Grace wasn't so sure about that assumption. Rye hadn't been in on this morning's meeting. Detective Nielsen didn't seem like a man who varied from the script in front of him, which told her that he might very well believe Brandon's claim of innocence.

"I want you to follow me back to my house," Rye said, not giving her a chance at rebuttal. "This way, your vehicle is safely ensconced between me and the agent assigned to protect you this evening."

Grace wasn't going to argue. There were too many loose ends, and she'd already been served up as the sacrificial lamb once. She sure as hell didn't want to be the next meal for the wolf.

"Okay," Grace replied softly, leaning over the console to receive a kiss. Her previous irritation had begun to wane, and she wanted nothing more than to curl up with him in front of the fireplace. Her desire reminded her that she needed to stop at her apartment before joining him at his place. "I've got to grab some clothes first, but then I'll be over."

"I can—"

Grace stopped Rye from saying anything else by pressing her lips to his. She'd meant to keep this brief, but his fingers somehow managed to slip underneath her bun and instantly sent shivers of arousal down her spine. The faint scent of his cologne enveloped them as her taste buds came alive with the delicious hint of mint that lingered from the treat at the end of their meal.

She leaned in closer, her breast pushing uncomfortably into

the console. She didn't care, though, as long as he didn't stop. Even after all this time, she couldn't get enough of him. Her wish was cut short by the ringing of his cell phone, and from the look on his face, it was clearly a client.

"Take it," Grace encouraged while taking advantage of this momentary clarity. She still had to stop at her apartment, and she didn't want to take too long knowing what was waiting for her. "I'll meet you back at your place."

"You can still follow me, so that you're safely in between two vehicles. Oh, and make sure to pack your black lace lingerie," Rye whispered with a lingering promise, stealing one more kiss before she leaned down to grab ahold of her purse she'd set on the floor mat. "You can leave the panties."

"And miss watching you take them off me?" Grace blew him a teasing kiss as she opened her door. "Not a chance."

"Charles, what can I do for you?" Rye asked at the same time he wagged a finger her way. "Friday? Yes, I'm sure we can…"

Rye was already deep in conversation by the time Grace closed the passenger side door. She waved as he pulled out and headed toward the exit, leaving her with her protective detail. She didn't doubt that he would be waiting at the exit of the garage. She reached into her purse for her keys, only to find that they weren't in the side pocket where she usually kept them.

Damn it.

Grace recalled setting her keys down on the credenza after having locked her filing cabinet for the night. She indicated to the driver in the vehicle who'd been tailing her all evening that she needed to go inside the building. Within seconds, a man she hadn't seen before stepped out of the car.

"Ma'am, is everything alright?"

"Yes, but I left my keys in my office." Grace began walking

toward the corner of the garage where the elevator was located in a small foyer. "I'm so sorry. I know this is probably an inconvenience."

"It's no problem, ma'am. I'm Jax Christensen. Ethan has the night off."

Jax opened the door for her, stepping back so that she could enter first. She wasn't in the least fooled that he hadn't already checked out the small enclosed area through the side window. There was an underlying tension in this man's shoulders that told Grace he was ready for anything or anyone.

Only one word could describe a man like him—dangerous.

She was glad he was on her side.

Without even knowing he'd done so, she found herself out of direct sight from anyone who could have been inside the elevator when the doors swooshed open. He then rested a hand on the side, preventing the doors from closing early as she stepped inside. She couldn't stop herself from quickly checking to see if he had a wedding band on his left ring finger.

He'd be the exact something needed to get Cynthia's mind off of Gareth.

Unfortunately, the man was sporting a thick silver ring that stated he'd been claimed.

Grace would have told him what floor her office was located on, but he'd already pressed the right button. Rye hadn't fooled around, had he? He'd hired the best of the best. It did ease her mind to know that someone was watching over them.

"Do you know if the security cameras are back up and running?" Grace asked, never having liked awkward silence in an elevator.

"Yes, ma'am. The garage owner had their security system completely tested and the video surveillance is now up and working properly."

"You can call me Grace." She offered him a smile, but he stepped in front of her as the elevator doors slowly opened to reveal the large area of the floor's lobby. It wasn't long until he indicated it was safe for her to vacate the elevator. His cautious behavior was somewhat alarming. "Is there something that I don't know about?"

"Not at all, Grace." Jax must have been listening to her earlier. "But you've basically had someone by your side the entire day, so it would have been rather hard for someone to make an attempt on your life. I don't know what to expect going into the offices of your place of business after hours, but my job is to ensure your safety. I'm just being cautious."

Well, when he put it like that…

"Wait. An attempt on my life?" Having someone try to frame her for murder was one thing, but to try and kill her? That was something else entirely. "There's something I don't know about, isn't there?"

"No," Jax answered confidently, though he came to a stop right before the glass doors of Manon Investments. "You know everything I do at this point, but is it usual for the door to be opened this time of night?"

"Yes." Grace continued through the opening, inhaling the mixture of leather and paper hanging in the air. Laurel said the scent reminded her of money, but Grace always thought it smelled like the interior of a brand-new car. "A few of the analysts work late hours, and Paul has been putting in at least fourteen-hour work days since Brad died. You can have a seat here. I won't be long."

It didn't surprise her when Jax didn't take her advice. Instead, he fell into step beside her as they made their way past Marilyn's desk and into the trading room. Grace was the one who stopped walking first.

"Steve, what are you still doing here?"

It was one thing for the analysts and the support staff to work late, but there was honestly no reason for Steve to still be sitting at the trading desk. He was still wearing the same clothes from yesterday, which told her that he never went home to change.

"Um, working. I was just going over some option trades that Smith is considering making on tomorrow's opening. Josh usually handled those types of trades." It was clear to Grace that Steve was doing nothing of the sort but staring off into space. As a matter of fact, he looked as if he'd lost his best friend. It didn't take a genius to figure out that he and Meredith hadn't patched things up. "What brings you back to the office?"

"I left my car keys here." Grace struggled with the decision to do what she came here to do, knowing full well Rye was going to be waiting for her near the exit of the garage, and taking a seat to get some type of reassurance that Steve had nothing to do with Brad's murder. After all, this was the perfect time. She had a personal bodyguard. "Steve, I heard about what happened with Meredith. I'm sorry."

Steve closed his eyes and inhaled slowly, clearly deciding if he should confide in Grace. Regardless that she wanted assurances, that didn't mean she couldn't be a friend in need. Josh was no longer here. His and Steve's friendship had been ruined due to choices that she wasn't sure he would retract if he could.

"Let me guess. Marilyn."

"You know that she's the eyes and ears of this office."

Steve shook his head in misery, most likely believing that he'd been betrayed on every level. Nothing in his life was going well.

"I didn't kill Brad."

Steve's declaration was said in anger, but his resentment was something she could understand.

"Neither did I," Grace responded softly, taking a seat in one of the rolling black chairs. Jax had judiciously given them privacy, though she could still see him standing near her office. "And trust me, being blamed for something so horrible can instill a rage inside of you that threatens to burn down everything in your life. But you can't let that happen."

"You think I'm a dick for what I did to Brad, don't you?"

"I know that Brad and Meredith were divorced." Grace set her purse down on the workspace in between two keyboards. "Who Meredith chose to spend her time with afterward is none of my business. It's no one's business but her own. Do I think you should have been the one to tell Brad? Yes, I do. Unfortunately, that's hindsight. What's done is done."

"But it's not done," Steve argued, leaning forward and squeezing the white and blue stress ball that he and Josh used to throw around the office on a daily basis. "Meredith had the audacity to ask me if I killed Brad in cold blood. You tell me. Did Rye Marshall ask you the same thing after your arrest?"

Grace wished she could share with Steve a similar story so that he didn't feel so alone, but she wasn't able to do that. Rye had never once doubted her, just as she hadn't him.

"My circumstances are different than yours, Steve," Grace shared reluctantly, not wanting anything she said to come out as vain. "I had a previous relationship with Rye to build on, along with having to overcome a lot of odds to be in the place we are now."

"This isn't just about Meredith and everyone here." Steve pressed his thumb and index finger against his eyes, though she doubted that it would relieve any of the built-up pressure. "My brother-in-law withdrew his bid to come work for Manon

Investments. And before you say anything, I know full well that the job offer was off the table the moment Brad's death became public knowledge. It's the point that his actions spoke louder than his words."

"Brad, I understand all too well how families fall apart under stress. My own mother closed the door in my face this evening after I went over there to speak with Brandon. He's the one who committed insider trading, was arrested for murder, and yet I'm the villain." Grace had calmed down a lot since she and Rye had driven away from the Walsh residence. She was able to put things in better perspective now that some time had passed. "What my family can't understand is that I'm not willing to compromise my integrity for the sake of smoothing over someone else's mistakes."

Damn, but it felt good to say that aloud.

"Steve, call Josh." Grace hoped that her brother had someone telling him something similar. It was doubtful, considering her mother was acting as his gatekeeper. She could still hope. "Josh was your friend, and you made a mistake by not telling him that you were seeing Meredith. Josh and Anita used to be pretty close with Brad and Meredith back in the day. I'm sure you can understand why he felt betrayed at being kept in the dark."

"You don't get it. Josh betrayed me the moment he went to Brad with his suspicions." Steve's defensive attitude was most likely what got him in this predicament to begin with. She should know, considering it was the reason she walked away from Rye in the first place. "Josh should have come to me first."

· "And how do you think Josh felt finding out from a stranger that you and Meredith were involved? You worked longer hours beside him than he spent with his own wife. Secrets like that can destroy even the strongest of friendships." Grace wondered if

her relationship with her family might have been different had
Brandon come and apologized to her and Rye for betraying
them. Would she have been a better person and forgiven him for
his crimes? Well, she doubted she would ever know that
outcome. "Call him, Steve. Make amends, because you need a
friend now more than ever."

Grace quietly stood and picked up her purse, astonished that
such a random conversation had helped her put things into
perspective with her own family. She'd harbored guilt over too
many things out of her control. She'd learned to leave remorse
behind with her experience with Rye, but she could now do the
same with her mother.

It didn't take her long to close the distance to her office. Jax
had already flipped on the light switch, so all she had to do was
cross the threshold to where her credenza was positioned on the
back wall.

There was only one problem.

Her keys were nowhere to be found.

CHAPTER ELEVEN

"DO YOU WANT another glass of wine?"

Rye waited for Grace to reply, but it was obvious she hadn't heard his inquiry. She'd been staring at the flickering flames of the blazing fire for the last ten minutes.

"Grace?"

Rye had no doubt she was going over this evening's events with a fine-tooth comb. He'd done so himself a hundred times in the past hour, but neither of them would find the answers they sought here in this moment.

He'd walked into Manon Investments just in time to find Grace holding her keys, but she'd been adamant she hadn't left them on her desk. Steve had sworn that he hadn't seen anyone enter her office, but he really couldn't have been sure given that the trading desk faced away from Grace's door.

Rye had driven to the exit of the parking garage, only to sit there finishing his conversation while staring into the rearview mirror waiting for Grace's car to pull up behind his. Only five minutes had passed with no sight of her. He wasn't about to leave the garage without her in between him and the agent assigned to her for the night.

Unfortunately, a vehicle had driven up behind Rye before he could put his car in reverse. He'd had no choice but to drive through the gate, around the block, and back into the entrance of the parking garage. Before he'd pulled his Audi alongside

Grace's car, the agent with her had sent a text that Grace had forgotten her keys.

"Did you know that an alien spaceship landed outside my office today?"

Grace didn't blink.

Rye did the only thing he could.

"Hey!" Grace exclaimed after he'd tried to pry her fingers off her wineglass. One would have thought he'd been trying to steal her jewelry. "Hands off."

"Now that I have your attention, would you like more?" Rye asked with a lift of the bottle.

"I'm sorry." Grace scrunched her nose in a sheepish manner. "I'm not very good company, am I?"

"You know, you could have easily knocked your keys on the floor and the cleaning crew set them on your desk after picking them up."

There could have been multiple reasons why Grace's keys weren't where she'd left them.

"The cleaning crew doesn't come into the office until after ten o'clock at night."

"Someone else could have been in your office leaving you a file."

"There were no files on my desk."

"Maybe someone was walking by and glanced into your office only to spot your keys on the floor." Rye would continue to offer scenarios until she accepted that there was most likely a simple explanation as to why her keys weren't in the spot she thought she'd left them. She'd been on edge ever since her arrest, though he didn't blame her. "Grace, for all we know, you forgot that you set the keys on your desk after locking the filing cabinet. We've all been under a lot of stress lately."

"Do you recall me setting my keys on my desk?" Grace

asked, shifting in her seat on the couch so that she could face him. She'd taken her blonde strands out of their confinement, allowing the silky tresses to hang over her shoulder. "You were there when I closed up my credenza. I remember setting my keys down next to the vase I have positioned in the middle, but then we began talking. The next thing I remember is grabbing my purse and walking out ahead of you."

Rye wished he could tell her that she was wrong, but he'd be lying if he said he could recollect her setting her keys on her desk. He reached out and wrapped one of the blonde strands around his finger. He never tired of touching her.

"I don't remember, angel, but that doesn't mean you didn't. We were both preoccupied with our intentions to speak with Brandon." Rye wondered when the time would come that their lives would return to normal, even a minor reflection of the time before he'd hired her stepbrother. "I do find it hard to believe that Detective Nielsen would allow a second arrest to happen with virtually no evidence. Someone tried to frame you for murder, so it wouldn't come as a surprise to find that someone attempted the same thing with Brandon when your situation didn't work out as he or she had planned."

"If the police would just arrest Brandon, I'd feel much better."

"Would you?" Rye countered, not knowing just how much more Grace's family could take in the wake of Brandon. He'd caused them a lot pain over the years, and this early parole was his one shot to turn things around. "I think if you really believed that, you wouldn't have gone to the trouble of writing down a list of suspects that I'm sure Detective Nielsen has already completely vetted."

Grace sipped her wine, but she didn't take her gaze off him in favor of the fire. As a matter of fact, those baby blue eyes of hers were burning a hole right through him. She always did have the talent of turning a conversation to another topic with a flip of a coin.

Rye didn't mind in the least, because he'd waited close to twenty-four hours for this moment. Hell, make that countless of years that dragged on without her presence. He finally got her back in his life, and that was where she was going to stay.

"I don't want to talk about Brandon, suspects, or the case anymore," Grace whispered, leaning in until their lips were inches apart. Her beauty never ceased to amaze him. "I said last night that I was going to let the police do their job. It's time for me to focus on what is truly important."

Rye had waited a very long time to be able to tell Grace that he'd never lost a drop of the love that had grown between them, not even when she'd searched for sunshine elsewhere. One of his foster mothers had told him that Jag had almost been adopted by a couple who thought having an older child might suit them. Unfortunately, they'd changed their minds when they caught sight of a four-year-old girl in pigtails.

He'd had been there when Jag was told of the change in plans, and neither one of them talked about the relief that had coursed through Rye's veins. There wasn't a need to do that when they'd still been together.

True love never died, no matter what form it was given.

"I've waited a very long time to tell you that I—"

The chime of the doorbell cut off Rye's overdue declaration.

"Why doesn't that surprise me?" Grace muttered, throwing her head back with a small groan. "Karma hates me."

"She doesn't hate you." Rye didn't bother to set his wineglass on the coffee table. He carried it with him to the door, though not before he made her laugh with his recollection. "And I could have sworn I heard Cynthia talking to you about karma the other day. Didn't she say to make karma your bitch or something to that effect?"

Rye was still cautious enough to look through the peephole regardless that the house was being watched by one of the agents from the Crest Security Agency. There were a lot of people who could have been standing on his front step, but never in a million years had he expected to see Gail Walsh.

For just a brief moment, he debated answering the door at all. Grace had been through the wringer today, and it certainly hadn't helped to be treated like an outsider by her own family. He honestly wasn't sure how much more Grace could take.

Speaking of karma...she was dishing shit out to Grace by the bucket load.

Rye looked over his shoulder to give Grace fair warning that their visitor wasn't here with chocolates and flowers.

"Bring it on," Grace murmured after draining the rest of the wine in her glass. He was glad she'd swallowed the smooth alcohol before he opened the door; otherwise, she would have spit it out all over the cushions of his cream couch. "Mom! What are you doing here?"

Grace scrambled off the couch, but Rye had already ushered Gail Walsh into the house. After what had happened a few hours ago, Grace probably wasn't in the mood for a lecture about wanting to speak with Brandon regarding the latest events. He'd never given Rye nor Grace anything but trouble since the very beginning.

"I, um...I came to apologize." Gail was dressed in the same black slacks she'd been wearing earlier. The burgundy silk blouse was tailored just so, and her jewelry definitely wasn't from a chain store. She'd married into money and nothing—absolutely nothing—was going to break the two apart. And that included Grace. "I was rather upset when you didn't come down to the station with me to support Brandon. He's been through a lot, but that didn't give me the right to treat you so rudely."

Heat flooded Grace's face as she stepped forward, most likely fully intending to list the hurdles that she and Rye had been left to deal with due to Brandon's actions. Rye had no choice but to put a hand out to stop her from raining hell down on the woman who'd given birth to her. Both would regret that type of exchange come morning.

"Gail, that's not much of an apology from where I stand." Rye was close enough to the fireplace that he was able to set his wineglass on top of the mantle. Anything with liquid was safer away from Grace's reach. The temptation to douse her mother might actually be too tempting. "Grace was framed for a murder she didn't commit. The police are suspecting Brandon not only of doing that, but also of being the guilty party of taking a man's life. I believe that it's Grace who's been put through a lot."

"Mom, what are you really doing here?" Grace wasn't giving an inch. Rye had always admired that she was independent and could stand on her own two feet when facing a battle. But she'd done that enough, especially in the past. He no longer wanted to be shoved into the background. It was time she understood that she didn't have to face anything alone. "And don't tell me it was to come and apologize, because we both know that's not true."

"But it is," Gail persisted, her blonde brows furrowing as she pursed her thin lips. Her gaze skimmed down and caught the fact that he'd had taken Grace's hand. A sad smile began to appear on beautiful features that gave Rye a glimpse into Grace's future. "I wanted so badly to support Brandon back then. He was young and reckless. He wanted to be noticed, and he did something that he'll regret for the rest of his life. I didn't handle the situation the way that I should have, and I thought it best you not even be in the same house as him, Grace. I didn't want to have to face what I'd done, and that wasn't fair of me."

Grace parted her lips as if she were going to argue every point Gail made in her admission. Rye lightly squeezed Grace's hand in hopes that she stopped long enough to really hear what her mother had just admitted to so long ago.

No parent was perfect.

Gail had handled a lot of things wrong in her quest to marry into money, but that didn't mean she didn't love her daughter. It was as obvious as the large diamond on Gail's left ring finger. The problem stemmed from Gail not knowing how to express that love without diving into the materialistic side of things.

"Brandon ruined my life, Mom." Grace continued to hold onto Rye's hand, and he had no problem being her rock for once. He hadn't been able to do so before, but they'd both promised to do things right this time around. "He ruined *our* lives and never bothered to show the slightest amount of regret. And you never once stopped to ask me if I was okay. Yesterday was only more of the same."

"Did you ever think to ask yourself why?" Gail's eyes filled with tears that she tried to blink away. "You have always been strong, Grace. Always. Brandon is like a little lost boy who can't find his baby blanket. All he wanted was security, and he went about achieving that goal in the wrong way."

"Security?" Grace asked with disbelief. "His father has enough money to see them through four generations. Don't excuse Brandon's criminal behavior because he thought those millions wouldn't be enough for him."

"And their arguments are for the record book, down to the very threat of Richard threatening to cut Brandon out of his inheritance and—"

Rye began to see where this was headed, so he finished Gail's statement.

"Your husband was able to control Brandon with the threat of leaving Grace everything should anything happen to the two of you."

It was more than apparent that Grace had never been a witness to those arguments. She was shaking her head in denial.

"Mom, I don't even get along with Richard."

"That's not true," Gail countered with a shake of her head that mirrored her daughter's. "You've always treated him with respect, you've never come to us for money, and you've become a successful businesswoman. Richard admires you, Grace."

"And that was all the more reason for Brandon to try and build a nest egg for himself, just in case Richard ever followed through on his threats." Rye was with Grace on this one, because nothing could excuse a grown man of consciously choosing to commit a crime. "What makes you believe that Brandon doesn't still harbor resentment against Grace?"

"Because all Brandon has talked about for weeks since he's been paroled were the different ways he could make things up to both of you," Gail shared, surprising both Rye and Grace when she closed the distance and stopped short not even a foot in front her daughter. "I thought letting you in the house earlier this evening would be a mistake because you were there to question his motives. I couldn't stand to see him slammed to the ground after having been at the police station almost eight hours the night before."

It was time for Rye to excuse himself. There were times a daughter needed her mother, and this was the first time either one had been honest with the other in a very long time.

"I'm going to go and make a few calls," Rye said softly, pulling Grace close so that he could press a gentle kiss against her temple. "You need this, angel. Take advantage of the moment."

Rye nodded toward Gail, giving her the respect she deserved

due to being the mother of the woman he loved. He'd yet to make that declaration to Grace, but his time would come. They'd waited this long; a little longer wouldn't hurt them any.

"Hey," Grace called out softly, catching his arm before he turned to walk out of the living room. There was relief in her baby blues, and something else—love. "Thank you."

Rye gave her a smile, but he hoped that she couldn't see it didn't reach his eyes. She needed this time with her mother, and he didn't want to take that away from her. Unfortunately, this evening had taken a turn neither of them had expected.

If Gail Walsh was certain that Brandon hadn't framed Grace for the murder he supposedly committed…then who had?

CHAPTER TWELVE

"Rye?"

Grace stood in the doorway of Rye's home office. The large area was saturated with the complete essence of him in every way. The rich tones of the walnut wood ran through his desk and numerous bookcases, and the highlights of the timber were brought out by numerous leather-bound books lined up symmetrically on the shelves. Even a small hint of his cologne hung in the air as if to welcome her into his domain.

"Are you coming to bed?"

Grace's mother had left a couple of hours ago, but Grace valued the much-needed time of mother and daughter. They'd both gone too long without it. Honesty was a beautiful thing, and not employed that much these days…even by family. They still had a long way to go to repair the damage done by the dysfunctional dynamics of two families brought together by marriage, but there was a light at the end of the tunnel.

Grace wasn't hiding her head in the sand that her mother placed a rather high value on the elite status of wealth. But everyone had flaws, and Gail Walsh's character defects could have been a whole lot worse.

The corporate world had taught Grace many things, but one stood out the most—being aware of a person's imperfections allowed her to limit her expectations.

"In a bit, angel." Rye was reading over something rather

intently, but he'd taken time to look at her with a tender smile. It wasn't long before he raised an eyebrow, clearly liking the fact that she was wearing one of his dress shirts...and nothing else. "I thought you would have fallen asleep by now. It was quite a day."

"Normally, I wouldn't have a problem falling asleep," Grace shared, walking across the cool hardwood floor to the large area rug that complemented the layout of his office. She gratefully sunk her toes into the plush material. "Someone has spoiled me, though. I'm used to you playing with my hair as I drift off to sleep."

Grace didn't miss the way Rye casually covered the piece of paper with his forearm.

"Rye, isn't that the list of suspects I created earlier this evening?" Grace wasn't upset that he'd taken it from her office, but she did have to wonder why. "We both agreed to let the police do their job."

"That was before we knew that Brandon didn't try to frame you for murder, or even worse, that he was responsible for killing Brad."

"What makes you think he didn't do it?"

"Because everything your mother said was true, right down to the fact that Brandon has daddy issues," Rye explained with concern, leaning back in his black leather chair now that she'd seen what he was working on this late at night. "It all makes sense, but what doesn't is that he would risk going back to prison all in the name of revenge. There's no motive here, which makes me believe that he was being used in the same manner you were as a patsy."

"Why us, though? The police are bound to believe there's a connection between Brad's murder and my family."

"Someone wants Detective Nielsen to believe that scenario.

Come here, angel." Rye rolled the chair back a bit so that she could walk around his desk, using the sturdy piece of furniture to lean against as he shared with her what had him so worried. "I thought back to what you said about the security system, the building's access, and the fact that someone had to have overheard your conversation with Laurel and Cynthia about the night Brad was murdered. You were the killer's easy way out."

"And Brandon happened to be a little too convenient. Talk about a gift landing in the guilty party's lap." Grace was glad when Rye reached for her hand. Being in a person's crosshairs who had no hesitation in taking a life in such a brutal fashion made her vulnerable. It also brought back memories she'd rather forget. "I've been used one too many times, Rye."

Rye would have stood to hold her in his secure embrace, but she laid a hand on the back of the seat to prevent him from doing so. She carefully straddled him until the wheels of the chair were secure against one of the bookshelves.

"Which is why going over this list wasn't such a bad idea," Rye shared, reaching up and brushing her hair so that the long strands hung down her back. "You work with these people, Grace. You're with those employees at least ten hours a day. Someone is capable of murder, and we're going to need to help the police as much as we can to get the focus off of you."

It wasn't in Grace's nature to think of those she cared about in such a horrible manner, which was why she'd struggled with the list in the first place. Everything Rye had said in the last few minutes was true, but she'd dealt with a lot this evening.

Right now, she wanted to focus on them.

She wouldn't make the same mistakes she'd made in the past, but like he'd said…their sights were now solely focused on the here and now. The past no longer mattered.

"What are you doing?" Rye whispered with a small smile,

knowing exactly what she had in mind. He lifted his lips to accept her soft kiss, and she didn't miss that his lashes lowered in arousal when she stroked his bottom lip with her tongue. "Those aren't angelic thoughts racing through your pretty head, are they?"

"Whatever do you mean, Mr. Marshall?"

Grace rotated her hips as she leaned in even closer, blowing gently into his ear before lightly catching his earlobe between her teeth. The fabric of his dress pants rubbed against her folds.

"I mean, we shouldn't start something here that we can't finish. I need—"

"This?" Grace murmured, leaning back enough to reach into the front pocket of the dress shirt she was wearing. She held up the foiled package in victory. "I've got your back, Rye."

"You've got more than that, angel. You've got my heart."

RYE PLUCKED THE condom out of her fingers before pulling her in close and kissing her until neither one of them could breathe. His cock hardened even more so than when he'd caught her standing in the doorway of his office. She was downright beautiful, and he always enjoyed the sight of her wearing only his dress shirt.

"Unfasten those buttons," Rye directed softly, reaching down to release the leather strap of his belt. "Show me your breasts."

Grace inhaled deeply, her trembling fingers reaching for the first button. Rye would never tire of hearing her breath hitch during intimate moments like this.

There were only three buttons that were fastened.

She slowly revealed her ample sized breasts, causing his dick to twitch inside the tight confines of his clothing.

"Touch your nipples." Rye barely got the words out, but she understood the directive. "Gently at first."

Rye continued to observe her as he drew down the zipper on his dress pants. His relief was fleeting, for the need to come at the sight of Grace throwing her head back at the pleasure of her own touch was strong. He denied himself, of course. This was a special moment to enjoy and endure.

He quickly tore the foil with his teeth before removing the disc from its holder. It wasn't long before his cock was covered with the latex, giving him the ability to run a finger through her folds.

"You're wet, angel."

"Hmmm," Grace moaned, shifting her hips forward to gain more contact with his hand. He drew his arm back, settling in to enjoy the show. "Rye…"

"Don't stop, Grace."

"Please."

"I want you drenched."

Grace began to tug on her nipples, her blue eyes darkening in arousal with each passing second. Her cheeks were naturally flushed from her own self-pleasure. The striking manner in which her lips parted slightly at the extreme sensations she was giving herself almost had him sinking inside of her, but he managed to control the urge.

"Is your clit swelling with the need to be touched?"

"Yesss," Grace practically hissed, catching her bottom lip between her teeth. She would have tilted her hips forward had he not put his hands on them to stop her. "Rye, I need—"

"To feel my cock slide into you? Do you need to feel full?"

Her nipples were now a darker shade from the continuous manipulation.

"I can't take the ache anymore, Rye. Make it go away."

Rye would have laughed had he the ability to, but playing with her in this manner meant stretching his own influence. There was only so much he could take himself, but he didn't have to do a thing other than hold the base of his shaft.

Grace had already used her knees to lift herself over the tip of his cock, and she sank onto him in one motion. The heat of her sheath was instantaneous. For a brief moment, he couldn't draw air.

"This," Grace whispered, releasing her nipples and using the headrest of his chair as leverage. She began to ever so slowly take the lead, which was what she needed after such an evening. Who was he to deny her the pleasure? "This is what I need, Rye."

"Then it's yours." Rye slid a hand behind her neck, bringing her closer so that he could kiss her. "You should know by now that I'm all yours, angel."

Grace built the momentum quickly, using her knees to force herself up and down as she took them to that special place. She once again tilted her head as the pleasure became immense. His sac began to tighten at the simple sight of her reaching…reaching…and finally attaining that elusive orgasm that catapulted his own.

"I love you," Rye managed to say after they both managed to calm their racing hearts after such a rush. "I always have, angel."

CHAPTER THIRTEEN

"PETER JENSEN CALLED from Morgan Stanley," Marilyn said as she walked around her desk with her usual water bottle. She'd had the same stainless steel cup for years. "He said there was a problem with the option trade Steve executed this morning."

"Thanks, Marilyn," Grace replied as she entered the foyer side by side with Laurel. "I'll call him back in a few minutes. Did Cynthia have an appointment? She was supposed to meet us at The Capital Grille for lunch, but she never showed and isn't answering her cell phone."

"Cynthia hasn't come out of her office since this morning."

Grace and Laurel shared concerned glances as they both veered down the hallway that would lead to Cynthia's office.

"That's not like her," Laurel muttered, not saying anything that Grace wasn't already thinking. Cynthia rarely stayed motionless unless there was a compliance-related issue at hand. "She seemed fine this morning."

Grace and Laurel had left the building before Cynthia due to Laurel needing to stop at Nicollet Mall to pick up a birthday gift for her mother. Cynthia had been on the phone and waved for them to go ahead, letting them know she'd meet them at the restaurant. They tried to get together in such a fashion at least once a month, because their work schedules were crazy.

"You don't think that—"

Grace had been going to bring up Gareth, considering he was the only one who seemed to be able to rattle Cynthia. Unfortunately, Paul stopped their progress down the hallway.

"Grace, could I see you for a moment?"

Had it been anyone else who'd requested a minute of her time when she was on a mission to ensure that her friend was okay, she would have turned him or her down flat. Unfortunately, Grace had been putting off having a discussion with Paul about her private life for some time now. There had been no need when she and Rye had been keeping their reconciliation a secret, but things had drastically changed given the events of the past week.

And last night?

Last night had been special in many, many ways.

"Go," Laurel said encouragingly, interrupting the direction Grace's thoughts had taken her. Laurel rested a hand on Grace's arm in reassurance before taking her purse so that she didn't have to carry it into her meeting with Paul. "Meet me in Cynthia's office when you're done."

Grace nodded her thanks before addressing Paul, though not before she saw Blair close her office door on the opposite side of the hallway. The quiet act of obtaining privacy didn't go unnoticed, and it also reminded Grace of what Rye had disclosed to her yesterday.

Paul and Blair had an affair, but it ended before she'd ever come to work for Manon Investments. Never once had either one of them been unprofessional in any way, shape, or form, but there was an underlying tension between the two of them that hadn't been there before Brad's murder.

Rye had asked Grace if anyone had been acting differently lately, and the answer came to her with a resounding yes. Blair's reaction to when Meredith had visited the office during Paul's speech had been hesitant, and Grace hadn't given the woman's conduct a second thought.

Now it made Grace reevaluate the situation.

Did Blair have something to hide?

"Of course, Paul." Grace gave him a smile as she fell into step beside him. "Is everything okay?"

"That's what I'm hoping you can tell me." Paul waited to start their conversation until they were in the sanctity of his corner office, completely opposite of where Brad's office had been located. The crime scene tape had been removed, but the door had remained closed ever since a special cleaning crew had come in to remove the bloodstains from the carpet. "A lot has happened since Brad's…untimely death."

Paul's hesitation on what really happened to Brad was understandable, given their friendship. He was still grieving. Grace expected him to be grieving for some time, because one didn't just get over the death of a friend.

"And you're doing an excellent job in keeping Manon Investments running until the deal with Smith goes through." Grace was well aware that Paul and Smith were meeting with clients and offering a seamless transition to Gallo Capital Management should they choose to stay in-house. "Is there something that I can do to help you?"

"You can reassure me that you're not going to leave Manon Investments for Marshall Securities."

Grace never had any intention of working with Rye, because she'd always been adamant they keep their professional lives separate from their personal affairs. Laurel and Smith were making it work, and Grace couldn't be happier for them.

That arrangement wasn't conducive to Grace and Rye.

"I've been meaning to have a talk with you, Paul," Grace expressed her sincerity, crossing her legs so that she was more comfortable in the chair. This conversation wasn't going to be quick, so she might as well settle in for the duration. "It wasn't my intention to put Manon Investments back in the spotlight with my arrest. The way the media handled—"

"Grace, I want you to know that I never believed for even a second that you killed Brad," Paul protested, having taken the other guest chair instead of walking around his desk. His weathered face wasn't as tanned as it had been weeks ago from his trip to the Caribbean. "There's nothing we can do with the coverage we've been getting in the press, other than ride out the storm. I'm not going to say I wasn't surprised to find that you and Rye Marshall were seeing one another, because it does bring up another question."

"I've already signed a non-disclosure agreement about the trades we execute, Paul." Grace didn't take offense to Paul's need for caution when it came to the hedge fund. "Cynthia had all of us sign non-disclosure agreements the moment she took over as compliance officer."

"I knew I hired that woman for a reason," Paul muttered, rubbing a hand down his face. It was then that Grace noticed the exhaustion written in his features. "I think we've covered everything then."

"Have we?" Grace hadn't meant to bring up the subject of the murder investigation, but everyone had to be thinking the same thing. "Paul, do you really believe that the guilty party isn't someone in this office?"

"I ask myself that question every minute of the damned day, Grace." Paul leaned forward and rested his elbows on his knees. "I can't bring myself to accuse anyone here. We know these people. We spend more time with those here at Manon Investments than we do our own families."

Grace could see that Paul would never truly accept that

someone they'd all trusted here at the firm could ever do something so horrendous. She smiled sympathetically, having had that very same mindset right before it was she who had cold metal being wrapped around her wrists.

"Look, I get it. I don't want to think anyone here is guilty, either, Paul." Grace stood and smoothed out her skirt, looking down at a man whose life had changed along with everyone else at this firm. She wished she could agree with him, giving him peace of mind, but she knew better now. "But it's more than obvious that someone here at Manon Investments is responsible for Brad's death. And whoever it was, he or she felt confident enough to try and frame me for his murder. So if you know anything at all that could help the police solve this case, then you should tell them."

Grace quietly left Paul where he'd been sitting, opening and closing his office door behind her. He had so much on his plate with keeping Manon Investments afloat until such a time that the assets could be taken over by Gallo Capital Management. She hadn't wanted to add to the load he was carrying, but she was done being used as a patsy for some insane individual who thought he or she was in the clear of spending the rest of his or her life behind bars.

"Cynthia, are you—"

Grace had been going to ask if Cynthia was alright, but the answer was clear from the shocked expression on her pale face. Her red lipstick didn't complement the shade whatsoever.

"Grace, close the door." Laurel had been kneeling in front of Cynthia, and it was apparent that whatever had happened was bad. "Quickly."

Grace spotted her purse on one of the chairs. She fought the urge to grab her cell phone and call Rye, because whatever Cynthia was about to say was bad…really bad.

"Tell me," Grace ordered them briskly, leaning against the office door after she'd closed it. She had a feeling she was going to need the support. Either that, or the bottle of wine Laurel had hidden somewhere in her office. "Get it over with. Did the police arrest Brandon?"

It was the only thing she could think of that would cause this reaction, though giving it a second thought...Cynthia would have made some offhand remark about the man and been done with it.

No, whatever had happened involved Cynthia personally.

Nausea rolled Grace's stomach in waves. Was Cynthia about to be arrested for Brad's murder? There was no way she would be able to go through the booking process. She'd end up assaulting one of the officers, only adding to the impending charges.

"No, this has nothing to do with Brandon."

Laurel had been the one to reply, because it appeared that Cynthia was still at a loss for words. That rarely happened. As a matter of fact, Grace had never witnessed such a thing.

"Then what?" Grace demanded, ready to come unglued at the thought of her friend suffering in such obvious horror. "Cynthia, what is it?"

"I was—" Cynthia struggled to find words, but she slowly inhaled and patted Laurel's hand to signal that she was okay. She wasn't, that much was clear, but she was gathering her composure. "I was cleaning out Brad's personnel file. I wasn't here when that paperwork was filled out at the start, and there was never a reason for me to look at it."

Grace shared a concerned look with Laurel, who was already in the know. Whatever Cynthia had discovered in that file was worse than Grace's arrest, and that was saying something.

"Who's going to be wearing orange?" Grace asked in a whisper, trying to inject a bit of humor in the mix like Cynthia usually would in these instances. The attempt failed miserably. "Just rip off the bandage, Cynthia. Who do you have to turn into the police?"

"Gareth." Cynthia practically choked on his name. "He lied to me. All this time…and he never told me the truth."

"The truth?" Grace wanted to cover her ears, but she would never let down her friend. She would have said she'd go buy the body bag and shovel, but they were already talking about murder. "Cynthia, maybe Gareth didn't have a choice but to keep you in the dark. I'm sure he has a reasonable explanation about whatever it was he lied to you about."

"A reasonable explanation?" Cynthia laughed, but there was no humor to be found. Grace's heart hurt for her friend, because this nightmare they'd found themselves in wasn't over. At least Grace had Rye to go home to, but Cynthia's next statement confirmed that she had no one. "The man I fell in love with was Brad Manon's brother, and Gareth had a major motive to commit murder."

~ THE END ~

Thank you for following along with the Office Roulette trilogy! Are you ready for the thrilling conclusion that will leave you on the edge of your seat?

http://www.kennedylayne.com/opportunity.html

USA Today Bestselling Author Kennedy Layne brings you the thrilling conclusion to the Office Roulette trilogy...

Gareth Nicollet had been born into wealth, but he'd learned at an early age that money wasn't everything it was cracked up to be. Regrettably, he'd made a meaningful choice early on in his life that now threatened his future with the woman he loved.

Cynthia Ellsworth valued many things, but trust and loyalty were at the top of her list. She'd always known the man who shared her bed had secrets, but she never thought in a million years that he had the ability to destroy her career and her heart with a single blow.

Someone once said that greed was balanced by fear, but that wasn't entirely true when there was nothing left to lose. Unfortunately, Gareth's secret is the very reason the roulette wheel is spinning and Cynthia's life hangs in the balance.

Books by Kennedy Layne

Office Roulette Series
Means (Office Roulette, Book One)
Motive (Office Roulette, Book Two)
Opportunity (Office Roulette, Book Three)

Keys to Love Series
Unlocking Fear (Keys to Love, Book One)
Unlocking Secrets (Keys to Love, Book Two)
Unlocking Lies (Keys to Love, Book Three)
Unlocking Shadows (Keys to Love, Book Four)
Unlocking Darkness (Keys to Love, Book Five)

Surviving Ashes Series
Essential Beginnings (Surviving Ashes, Book One)
Hidden Ashes (Surviving Ashes, Book Two)
Buried Flames (Surviving Ashes, Book Three)
Endless Flames (Surviving Ashes, Book Four)
Rising Flames (Surviving Ashes, Book Five)

CSA Case Files Series
Captured Innocence (CSA Case Files 1)
Sinful Resurrection (CSA Case Files 2)
Renewed Faith (CSA Case Files 3)
Campaign of Desire (CSA Case Files 4)
Internal Temptation (CSA Case Files 5)
Radiant Surrender (CSA Case Files 6)
Redeem My Heart (CSA Case Files 7)

Red Starr Series

Starr's Awakening(Red Starr, Book One)
Hearths of Fire (Red Starr, Book Two)
Targets Entangled (Red Starr, Book Three)
Igniting Passion (Red Starr, Book Four)
Untold Devotion (Red Starr, Book Five)
Fulfilling Promises (Red Starr, Book Six)
Fated Identity (Red Starr, Book Seven)
Red's Salvation (Red Starr, Book Eight)

The Safeguard Series

Brutal Obsession (The Safeguard Series, Book One)
Faithful Addiction (The Safeguard Series, Book Two)
Distant Illusions (The Safeguard Series, Book Three)
Casual Impressions (The Safeguard Series, Book Four)
Honest Intentions (The Safeguard Series, Book Five)
Deadly Premonitions (The Safeguard Series, Book Six)

About the Author

First and foremost, I love life. I love that I'm a wife, mother, daughter, sister... and a writer.

I am one of the lucky women in this world who gets to do what makes them happy. As long as I have a cup of coffee (maybe two or three) and my laptop, the stories evolve themselves and I try to do them justice. I draw my inspiration from a retired Marine Master Sergeant that swept me off of my feet and has drawn me into a world that fulfills all of my deepest and darkest desires. Erotic romance, military men, intrigue, with a little bit of kinky chili pepper (his recipe), fill my head and there is nothing more satisfying than making the hero and heroine fulfill their destinies.

Thank you for having joined me on their journeys...

Email:

kennedylayneauthor@gmail.com

Facebook:

facebook.com/kennedy.layne.94

Twitter:

twitter.com/KennedyL_Author

Website:

www.kennedylayne.com

Newsletter:

www.kennedylayne.com/newslettertext.html

www.ingramcontent.com/pod-product-compliance
Lightning Source LLC
Chambersburg PA
CBHW072029170626
46811CB00008B/2998